David Schnei

Don't Kill Me- I'm Only The Entertainer!

**David Schneider
c.2012 Eko Press**

<u>For Debi and for Dad</u>

This is a work of FICTION…sort of.

It was 1980- the start of a new decade…

Those that dance are often considered insane by those who cannot hear the music.

-George Carlin

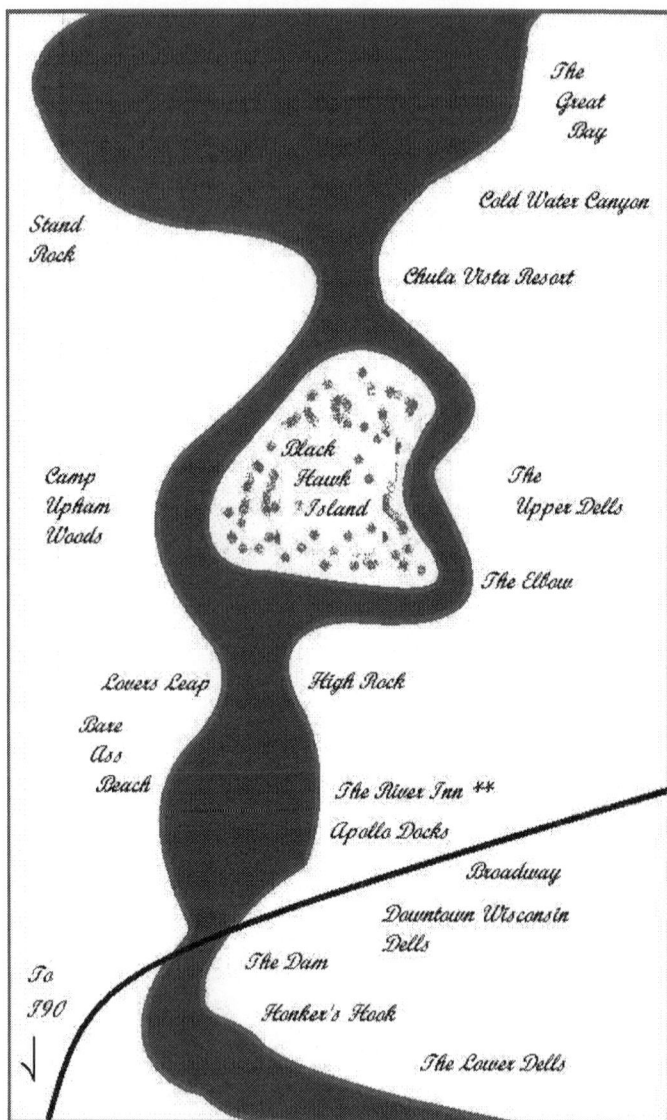

dell (del) *n.* a small, deep valley; a hollow.M.E. *delle,*

1.

"They told me the streets were all paved with gold- but these dirty sidewalks are gray concrete floors...."

-C. Weil

The Vogues were crooning a classic as Schneider walked through the glass doors and tripped down the steps to the rest of his life. It was 10:48 on a Friday morning in June. He dusted himself off and was immediately struck by the view.

Beyond the empty barstools a row of picture windows revealed a mid-morning sun depositing a million diamonds in the middle of the river. They spread out until halted by vertical red cliffs on both banks, and before them, Schneider could see the sandstone walls flatten out to form a sandy beach.

"Where's the magic in this magic town..."

Where was the magic? He was looking at it. Barely out of high school, he wondered how he would ever compete with the river itself.

Surely everyone would simply pick up their cocktails and stroll out to the deck and the tiki torches, never to be seen again.

Schneider turned to the tiny stage situated between the staircase and lower level where the bar was. On the wall behind it hung two oil paintings: they both showed the river's signature rock formation. On the left, a modern tour boat threaded through it. On the right, a paddlewheel steamboat from the turn of the century.

Just like the postcards.

Alone in the lounge, Schneider lifted a stool off the empty bar and carried it past the blaring 45-filled jukebox to the stage. He sat down and pondered the view, which would be his for a summer's worth of evenings.

That view. Most of his friends would be spending the summer in Madison flipping burgers on the main drag or hosing sausage makings off the floor during the graveyard shift at the Oscar Meyer plant. He smiled again.

Fresh river air wafted in through the open door leading from the deck and mingled with the interior scent of bar mix, stale beer and disinfectant. Dominating all this was the pleasing aroma of beef slow roasting in the kitchen. He was about to start unloading his gear when the door to the kitchen bumped open and in walked Seering, whining a Neil Young tune to compete with the Vogues.

"'…with a cinnamon girl'- Schneids you made it! We just got the Prime in the oven for tonight."

"Jesus, Seering, I almost forgot about those steps," offered Schneider, looking up towards the door.

"What do you mean?" asked Seering.

Schneider shook his head, dismissing it and nodded towards the windows.

"This is even nicer in the summer," Schneider said.

His thoughts returned to December, when he had recruited two friends from the University of Wisconsin swing choir- the keyboard player and the lead singing bombshell- to help him provide entertainment for a holiday party Seering had booked there. Schneider would sing and play drums.

Until Seering had taken over the resort's management that autumn, The River Inn had spent the winter months boarded up, as had most of the area's hotels and restaurants. Seering was one of the first to see winter recreation and corporate entertainment as a way to boost cash flow for the struggling business during the off-season.

He had opened ten rooms on the third floor of the historic Inn for the holiday party, one of which he then offered to Schneider.

All Schneider could remember of that night was the entire swing choir, complete with orchestra, showing up midway through the second set. Everything after that was a blur, until waking up the next morning- in a closet. Four people of various sexes and stages of undress slept in his bed. More had been scattered around the floor.

He had noticed his hands had cuts on them and his clothes from the night before were a mess.

"What the hell happened last night?" he had croaked after stumbling downstairs to Seering's hotel apartment. He held out his hands.

"I don't know," replied Seering, "but I think you cut your hands on the symbols during that second encore- Jeez Schneids, I thought the whole stage was gonna vibrate into the river- and all those suits drooling over that blonde singer- I've never seen anything like it!"

Seering had handed him a mug of hot coffee and turned to finish a pitcher of Bloody Marys. Schneider cupped his hands around the coffee and walked into the living room.

The French doors leading from the porch were thick with frost. Bright morning sunlight and frigid cold air blowing off the river had seemed to compete for entry into the cozy room. A fire had blazed in the old wood burner.

"Never seen anything like it," Seering had repeated from the apartment's tiny kitchen.

"Yeah," Schneider had muttered. "I wish I'd been there."

"I gotta find it girl, before I bring you to... this magic town."

That had been quite a weekend, and now, jerked back to the present, Schneider was wondering what three *months* in this place during the peak summer tourist season would do to him.

He couldn't wait.

****

The year was 1945. The war was winding down in the western Pacific. In the Eastern Pacific- San Francisco Bay to be exact, the U.S.S. Yakatuk and U.S.S. Half Moon sit in dry dock at Hunters Point Naval Shipyard. Their crews sit shore-side with little to do.

Seaman Robert Schneider and Seaman James Seering, by virtue of the fact their last names both start with the same letter, found themselves on the same details, and muster lists. The war was five thousand miles away, and boredom was the main enemy here. Seaman Schneider decided he was a warrior. Stamping out this enemy was his sacred duty and nothing would stand in his way. Not even the base commander.

During World War II, short sheeting had become a worn-out naval tradition and Schneider wanted to try a new twist on an old theme. At the same time, Schneider was growing tired of the way his CO was running things. So stodgy- so...*military*. After all, the world was celebrating VE day. So instead of merely redoing the sheets on the Old Man's bunk, Seaman Schneider decided to hang the entire bed out his base apartment's third floor window.

The CO was not amused and the next morning's muster found him screaming ultimatums at the entire crew.

"The guilty party will step forward or there will be no liberty as scheduled*!!*"

It was right out of *Mister Roberts*.

Standing at attention down the line, Seaman Seering knew, as everyone else did, who the guilty party was. He also knew that one more transgression and Schneider was out. Schneider couldn't very well take that step forward, so Seering took it for him. The CO never really believed Seering had done it, but the liberty was extended and Seering and Schneider became fast friends.

It turned out that they were both from Wisconsin and had similar interests, namely hunting, fishing, and getting the hell out of the Navy. They and their ancient mine sweepers were already out of the war.

They went home to Wisconsin and built a thirty-year friendship. Schneider earned a Business degree on the GI bill from the University of Wisconsin, and married a pretty, petite church choir director. Seering went on to law school.

All went well until the spring of 1964 when Schneider's 6 year-old son David woke up on a morning they were to visit his grandparents and walked out to their kitchen. He giggled when he saw his mother lying on the kitchen floor, thinking it was time to play a game.

The cerebral aneurysm left the Schneider family without a wife and mother. For a short while after, they spent almost every weekend at the Seerings. Jim and his wife Jean had three children, Jill, Jeff, and Dan- Dan being the oldest.

There was seven years difference between young David and Dan, but throughout the 1960's David Schneider would store away many mental snapshots of Dan Seering.

"So, ferry- 'cross the Mersey, 'cause this land's the place I love…"
                    -Jerry & the Pacemakers

Among those images was the Rec room in Seering's home where Dan and David's older sister Debi would spend hours listening to a Sears record player blaring stacks of 45s. Dan had rigged the entire room with multi-colored lights that pulsated to the beat of the music. There was a small refrigerator that was always stocked with glass bottles of *Coke*, *Orange Crush,* and *Dr. Pepper.*

Next to the fridge, Dan had rigged a dartboard to rotate on an electric motor, making the game a little more interesting- then had hung his girlfriend's bikini on it. Boredom was still the enemy- but a brand new generation was picking up the gauntlet.

That same summer, at the northwoods lake where the Schneiders and Seerings both owned vacation cottages, David would remember the day that Dan's old wooden runabout- Dan loved boats- caught fire in the middle of Lake Eleanor. The boat had been anchored after some water-skiing; the music of Jerry and the Pacemakers drifted from the AM radio across the lake. In the boat were Dan, Dan's best friend Dave Wright, Debi Schneider, and her friend Katy.

Schneider remembered hearing the gas explosion and turning to see the boat engulfed in flames. The boys immediately sprang into action, heroically dousing the fire with wet towels and buckets of water- then casually laid back on the bow of boat and let the girls row them back to shore.

There was a certain style exhibited here, young David realized then. Boats and music. David would grow up fascinated by both.

Meanwhile, Dan Seering turned his interest in things nautical into a summer job, getting a Captain's license between semesters at the University of Wisconsin at Madison and piloting a tour boat for Dells Boat Company (DBC) on the scenic "Lower Dells" of the Wisconsin River.

The "Dells" of the river was separated into two sections: the Upper Dells above the small hydroelectric dam and the Lower Dells below the dam.

One sunny afternoon while approaching the shallows near the outflow of the dam, a pretty girl in a pink halter-top came forward to ask Seering a question. The question evidently had little to do with the river or the tour.

When Seering finally looked back to where he was going, he heard a sickening crunch, and the hundred-passenger excursion boat ground to a halt, high and dry on the rocks below the dam. It was the only time in the town's recorded history that the power company had to open the dam to re-float a tour boat.

Despite the incident, Seering would develop a deep love for that river and, after earning an MBA, he would return to manage an historic but ailing river resort on the Upper Dells, just above the dam. Seering felt he would need two things to attract patrons back to the once popular resort: One was great food. He would have to hire a superb chef to run the dining room and kitchen. The other was live entertainment.

Seering remembered hearing the Schneider kid singing and playing his guitar around the campfires at the cottage. The kid could certainly sing, and he was in his last year of high school so he'd be cheap too. Seering would ask if Schneider wanted to play a small party at the resort during the off-season, and if that went all right, maybe a job playing in the lounge for the summer. He'd offer him room, board, and a small salary.

And Seering, never missing a trick, would later mention the alternating weekend duties of AM dishwasher and PM janitor as an aside, as if it had always been part of the deal.

"They say the neon lights are bright on Broadway..."

-C. Weil

After some small talk in the River Inn's lounge, Dan Seering took David Schneider up to the second floor to show him his room for the summer, and then Schneider went out to the car to unpack his first load of sound gear. He was supposed to play that evening, so it was best he got started. He figured he'd set up, get some lunch, and look around town. Then he'd come back and do a sound check before the dinner crowd started wandering in.

As he walked up River Road and across the bridge, he glanced down and saw the Apollo steamboat, a second-generation cousin of the old paddle wheeler depicted in the painting in the River Inn's lounge, resting at her dock.

The current steamer still paddled tourists up and down the river, always demanding the attention of everyone on the river but seldom full herself. Watching her rest at her moorings seemed to turn the clock back 50 years.

As he neared town and the main drag, however, Schneider could sense quiet history fading and loud tackiness looming.

Wisconsin Dells, Wisconsin was a town that all of a sudden *was just there*. It grew up at the turn of the century as a rest stop for loggers guiding massive rafts of raw timber from the dense northern forests to the mill towns in the south. They needed the rest after negotiating the narrows that were formed by the spectacular rock formations of the area. These narrows created fast water with unforgiving currents, and many a man lost his life here. The town was then known as Newport.

The Ho-Chunk Winnebago Indian nation also resided here. Years ago, they had used the sandy soil and natural river transportation to their considerable benefit. Today, their main income was derived from the nightly ceremonial dancing at *Stand Rock,* which they had shrewdly turned into one of the town's main tourist attractions.

The *Dells* now existed principally as a playground for Chicago and northern Illinois vacationers and was responsible for what the locals termed the *Friday Chi-town shuffle-* a mass of north-bound vehicles entering Interstate 90 around 5PM and clogging it up until turning off at exit 92 or 88. Then they would proceed to clog up the one road that those exits led to- The *Strip*, a three mile-long ribbon of billboards, hotels, T-shirt shops and water slides.

Then it was over the River Bridge, where the Strip narrowed to two lanes and spilled a hundred station wagons and two hundred Cadillacs per hour onto the main drag itself.

Broadway or '*The Drag*' as it was known to locals, was much like The Strip, except on every corner stood the ubiquitous River Tour ticket stand, where every pitch imaginable was employed to turn strolling tourists into floating tourists.

Most of the ticket booths were manned by college kids just "trying to pay their way through school" and have some fun.

They all learned their trade from the *River Rats-* veteran river pilots that returned year after year for a lifetime, unable or unwilling to outgrow the party.

Schneider walked up Broadway, past bars and wax museums, old-time photo galleries and moccasin shops. He stopped to read a sign that simply read *"Ride the Ducks."*

He pondered what the hell a *"Duck"* might be until nearly being run over by one. Stumbling back from the curb, he studied the ass-end of this duck, which was obviously in a hurry to get somewhere.

So that was a *Duck*.

He remembered reading about the amphibious vehicles used in World War II and how some of them were converted to other uses after the war. Evidently these Ducks couldn't resist the party either, judging from their multicolored stripes and cute canopies.

There seemed to be an infinite number of ways to redistribute Chicago's wealth into the local Dells' economy.

After passing the offices of Dells Boat Company, he turned off the main drag and headed back towards the River Inn. Walking along, Schneider wasn't so sure that the "Ducks" and the "Rats" didn't have the right idea. He remembered Seering saying that Wisconsin Dells wasn't a town- it was a lifestyle, a mood. There was a *freedom* here. A sense of *anything goes*. And the dollars were definitely flowing north- not the other way around.

"The first time... ever I saw your face..."
-Roberta Flack

When he returned to the River Inn for his sound check, Schneider saw a young woman sitting on the same barstool that he had deposited on the little stage earlier. She was tuning a guitar. As Schneider carefully descended the last step of the lounge and turned toward her she opened her mouth to sing and Schneider froze in his tracks. He gaped. Her voice was as beautiful as she was. He felt as if he had just drunk two martinis. Who was this girl?! And what was she doing here?

He sat down at the nearby service bar and waited for her to finish. She gave him a smile that would melt titanium, then suddenly stopped and introduced herself.

"You must be the manager. I'm Liz, your entertainment for the summer."

****

Schneider couldn't contemplate the obvious smart-ass replies that would have gone through most American males' minds at that point. Instead, all he saw was burgers and broomsticks and having to drive back to Madison without a summer job.

Where was Seering? If that idiot had promised his summer gig to this-- vision sitting before him, and then forgot to tell him he'd kill him. What the hell had happened?!

"Are you sure you're in the right place?" stammered Schneider.

"This *is* the River Inn, right?" replied Liz. "I was here last week when the owner signed my contract."

The owner? "Which owner?" managed Schneider. He remembered meeting both partners at last winter's party. One was a great guy. One was not.

"Bob King," said Liz. She handed Schneider the contract, then raised her eyebrows.

Raven hair against flawless dark skin offset by a well-filled white cotton blouse. Her eyes were blue, and they looked right through him.

"You *are* the manager, right?" she asked.

"Well, not exactly- *SEERING*!!"

The kitchen doors swung open and Dan appeared carrying a vat of homemade margarita pre-mix and a cocktail tray full of ashtrays, still steaming from the Hobart. He placed the premix in the bar cooler.

"Yeah Schneids," he said while placing the ashtrays on each table in the lounge. He walked over to the jukebox and slid in a quarter. "Finished your sound check yet?"

The quarter clicked through the machine and sent The Beatles' *Help* careening through the speakers. Schneider nearly doubled over. Liz looked first at Seering then swung around to face Schneider.

"Why would *you* do *my* sound check?" Her smile now appeared capable of piercing armor- not merely melting it. Seering walked over and introduced himself to Liz.

"Schneids, I'm sorry I forgot to tell you earlier. King hired Liz here to play the cocktail crowd and then you come on at nine and play 'til bar time. Fair enough?" He looked at both of them.

"Sure," said Schneider, his immediate future suddenly brighter than ever.

"Maybe Liz and I can work up a half hour to do together for a transition- that OK with you Liz?" At that moment Schneider could think of no better way of spending the summer than singing love songs with this woman.

"Why not," she replied.

"Great," said Seering. "We open in an hour. Schneids, go clean up. You look like shit."

2

**"Scotch and Soda, mud in your eye,
baby do I feel high…"**
-The Kingston Trio

When Schneider came carefully back down the steep stairs later that night, the River Inn's lounge was half full and filling up. Cigarette smoke hung in the air. Every now and then the doors to the deck would swing open, and someone would head out to the river and those tiki torches, allowing a wee bit of haze to filter out.

Schneider was hungry and the deal was salary *plus* room and board. Since the former was a joke, he would at least take advantage of the latter. Schneider headed for the kitchen.

The Kingston Trio may have been playing in the lounge, but the kitchen was strictly rock and roll.

"You're as cold as ice!!…"

Someone was screaming along to *Foreigner* as Schneider approached the ovens.

"I'll have the Prime Rib and a glass of Burgundy," he announced.

"Schneider, get the hell out of here!" thundered Seering from the walk-in freezer. Schneider turned to comply and nearly flattened a waitress carrying a tray with service for six over her head. He would have to be a bit more careful in the future.

"Wait a minute Schneids- I want you to meet someone," said Seering. "Schneids, this is Dale Ryker, our executive Chef.

Ryker dropped his meat thermometer, finished his anthem to rock n'roll heartbreak, and extended his hand.

"Daylock Von-Scrotum the Third- how the hell are ya?" Ryker was wearing a tall chef's hat over closely cropped blonde hair. His blue eyes beamed through coke bottle- thick glasses.

"Fine, I'm doing... fine" responded Schneider. He resisted the reflex to wipe his hands on his slacks after Ryker released his vice-like grip.

"Interesting   nickname," gulped Schneider, not quite knowing what to say next.

"What nickname?" deadpanned Ryker. "Sorry, I got some meat needs tending… *Ain't that a shame…*"

Cheap Trick's updated version of The Big Bopper's golden oldie replaced Foreigner on the kitchen's radio as Seering guided Schneider out of the kitchen and into the dining room. He deposited him at a table as far from the kitchen doors as possible.

"Look Dave, I know the entire menu is open to you, but try and be a little more diplomatic when ordering, ok? And do it from a table- remember, that's the kitchen staffs' domain," he said, pointing to the doors they had just come out of. "As far as they're concerned, you've got a dream job- don't push it." Seering was smiling, but he was looking him right in the eye. Schneider couldn't remember the last time Seering had called him by his first name. It seemed awfully formal coming from him.

At that point Schneider realized for the first time he was speaking to the boss. His friend seemed comfortable in the role- even a natural, and he was all business now. It would still take some getting used to however.

"Ok," said Schneider. "I just have one question. Where the hell did you dig up your *executive* chef?" Seering grinned and stood up.

"Ask me again after your dinner. Stay out of trouble, OK Schneids?"

Schneider could hear Liz starting her second set in the lounge so he headed over.

Might as well wait for dinner in there, he thought.

As he entered the lounge his eye caught a familiar face at the bar next to the waitress station. The bartender, a local river rat of legendary status named Mike was pouring him a Windsor on the rocks, which confirmed his identity. Schneider walked over to him.

"Dave, how are you?" Dave Wright turned and beamed a grin that you could patent.

"Schneidy, good to see you!" They shook hands warmly. Schneider hadn't seen much of Dave Wright in years past, but Wright was the kind of guy you could meet once or a thousand times and every time you talked, it was like putting on an old favorite pair of jeans.

Wright was one of Seering's oldest friends. In addition to the Lake Eleanor boat fire, they shared many memories. They had roomed together in college during the early seventies, when classes might or might not be held depending on the intensity of the Vietnam War protests, and the Campus Police's reaction to them that particular day.

Seering remembered Wright coming back to their frat house early one cold November morning and announcing that Physics had been postponed- due to lack of a building. Someone had blown it to bits the night before, taking a 32 year- old math researcher with it. Evidently the Army had maintained a research lab in the building. Wright and Seering endured, finishing school while sharing piloting duties on the river during the summer months.

Wright had earned a degree in journalism. Schneider always figured him to be a writer. A cerebral, soft-spoken gentleman of spirit that could never resist a little hell raising, Wright enjoyed recounting the riverboat stories of years past. He had been on board as a guide during the now infamous "Seering-and -the babe-by- the-dam" fiasco.

Later, he would become a river pilot and Duck driver.

It had not all been strictly fun and games. One summer Wright had been piloting his tour boat when an overloaded fishing boat capsized and sent an overweight family of six into the river. None of them were wearing life jackets. The old loggers used to say that the Dells of the Wisconsin River was like a woman. The prettier she got, the more dangerous she became. The sheer cliffs that gave this area of the river its appeal also created bottomless pools with deadly currents hidden beneath its breathtaking beauty. You could make love to this woman if you chose the right time and place. Stumble around her, demand your own terms, however, and she could bite you, giving no second chances.

Wright had made sure his guide had control of the boat and the passengers, then dove in and saved all but one. That body was never found. The wire services picked up the story and Wright became an instant hero. But you'd never know it to ask him.

Someday, Schneider figured, Wright would be published in *National Geographic* or *Atlantic Monthly*. For now though, he was content to work at a local youth summer camp while sending out resumes and tending his journal.

"I thought I'd come over and see your big debut," said Wright. "Dan and Nemo and I are supposed to have dinner- have you seen them?" he asked while sipping his Canadian whiskey.

"Yeah, Seering just balled me out for poking my nose in his kitchen. Haven't seen Nemo yet though."

"*Wright, party of three, Wright party of three*" the voice over the PA system was sexy enough to make Wright do a double take at the overhead speaker. He gave Schneider a *did you hear that?* look and stood up.

"Send Nemo in *if* he shows up- you know Nemo. Stay out of trouble Schneidy- and break a leg."

Why was everyone always telling him to stay out of trouble? Wright's vacated barstool was the only one open, so Schneider hoisted himself up and ordered a tonic and lime. As he did so, an ornery looking guy three stools down looked at him as if Schneider had just stole his bar change. Well-dressed and tanned, around forty, the guy was talking with some buddies.

He reminded Schneider of a Mafia enforcer without the oil. A short teamster in an Izod sport shirt. The guy next to him looked just as mean but was much, much bigger. Now they were both staring at him. Pesci and DeNiro. If looks could kill, Schneider would have never known what hit him.

"...Rusty, I'm worth waiting for..."
                    - Liz

Schneider tried to manage a smile, then turned to listen to Liz. There was something magnetic about her. She had mentioned that she wrote her own material when they had talked earlier. Schneider listened. Her lyrics were full of optimism and self-confidence, but she didn't seem to flaunt anything. It was just *there*. She and Schneider were supposed to meet in the morning to go over some possible duets. Schneider was looking forward to it.

His drink came and when he turned to accept it he noticed that the Izod Enforcer was still giving him the eye. *Jesus- what was this guy's problem?* Schneider's first night working in a bar and it might be his last.

"Colsen, party of four- Colsen, party of four..." the sexy deep voice oozed again from the speakers. Schneider hadn't met the hostess yet but wondered if she looked as good as she sounded.

In response to the page, Izod Enforcer and his entourage stood up and headed for the dining room. *Who was this guy? And why does he want to kill me?* thought Schneider. He motioned to Mike the bartender, who was filling three margarita glasses at the far end of the bar. Mike placed them on a tray, added a tumbler half-filled with Dewer's and ice and brought the tray over to the waitress standing at the service bar.

"I think I'm making enemies here and I haven't sung a note." Lamented Schneider.

"Oh yeah? Not a good sign. Liz is doing great though- too bad you don't look like her." Mike turned to enter the bill for the drinks on a running dinner tab.

"I can't do much about that," responded Schneider. *At least the audience will change from week to week,* he reasoned to himself. *In this place, if you get a bad crowd one night, or someone makes things difficult, you can figure that come Monday, they're probably back in Chicago or Peoria making life miserable for someone else.*

"Well, I wouldn't worry about it too much," Mike said through his blonde handlebar mustache. "It's the locals you gotta impress around here. The opinion leaders, the ones that'll bring in the others week in and week out. Get *them* on your side and you can tell the weekend warriors to jump in the river. Who is the asshole, anyway?"

Schneider motioned to the party of four heading out to the dining room and pointed to Izod Enforcer, who was flicking a fly off the alligator over his breast pocket.

"Great job, Schneider," grinned Mike as he wipe-dried the frozen drink pitcher.

"You just pissed off the Mayor."

****

Dinner was served by a pretty waitress with dark hair and a flagrant bust. Her name was Kathy. It turned out she was from Madison, had gone to high school at a cross-town rival of Schneider's, and was a distant cousin of a close friend.

Kathy, Liz and Tammy-another friend from school- had all driven up together from Madison the previous month to apply for work in the area. They had all been offered jobs at the River Inn and decided to stay together. All were enrolled at the University at Madison for the fall semester, Kathy and Tammy majoring in Graphic Arts, Liz in Music. Schneider ate at the bar. He couldn't get over the quality of the music he was hearing. He had sung with a few singers-male and female- but this voice was special.

First it was haunting, then it was sweet. Then later, taunting and sexy. It had a certain style- an *insight*- and it was effortless. My God, this girl had *the package*- beauty and talent that could take her anywhere and the self-confidence that would allow it to happen.

Schneider couldn't decide on which level he was evaluating her, personally or professionally, so he decided to just eat.

He stopped in the middle of his first bite. The Prime Rib was the finest thing he'd ever tasted. If he could eat like this for the entire summer it would be worth the lousy salary. Where did Seering find this Ryker nut?

Schneider looked up to see Phil Waggel, another old friend of Seering's approaching from the stairs. With some irritation, he noticed that Waggel had no problem negotiating the "Stairway from Hell." Tall, dark, and more than happy to take advantage of it, Phillip "Nemo" Waggel approached the bar, and pulled out his money clip.

"Evening Nemo- some stairs, huh?" Schneider called across the bar.

"Hi, Schneids. What do you mean?"

"Never mind. Wright and Seering are waiting for you in the dining room."

"Thanks Schneids," said Waggel, lifting the glass of Johnny Walker Red that Mike had poured before Waggel had even reached the bar. Waggel walked over to Schneider.

"So this is the big night- who's the singer?"

"Name's Liz."

 Nemo inclined his head.

"All that and she can sing too? Sharing the bill, huh Schneids? How late does she play?

"'Till nine. Then it's me 'til close."

Waggel sipped his Scotch. "Did Dan tell you we bought a boat?" he asked.

Another Dells veteran, Waggel had spent his summer vacations years ago leaning out of the ticket booths up on Broadway, pitching tickets to the hordes of tourist that would inevitably board one of the boats that Seering and Wright and the rest of the "Newport Navy" were driving down on the river. Schneider had no doubt that Waggel's salesmanship had more than a little to do with DBC's success. Now, Waggel sold silos and tractors for International Harvester. God help the Mid-West farmer's daughters.

It seemed that Nemo and Seering and the rest of the boys, however, just couldn't get the river out of their system, so they had bought their own boat. A party boat. A *pontoon* boat.

"We're taking her out to Bare Ass Beach tomorrow," said Waggel.

"What's Bare Ass Beach?" Schneider inquired.

Waggel looked at Schneider as if he was about to explain the eighth wonder of the world to his own son.

"Schneidy," he said, "you see those two cliffs straight ahead?" He turned Schneider's barstool 180 degrees so Schneider could see up-river through the windows.

"The one on the right is *High Rock.* The one on the left is *Romance Cliff.* Now just this side of *Romance Cliff*- see the beach?" Schneider nodded.

"That's Bare Ass."

"How'd it get the name 'Bare Ass Beach'?" "Well, a few years ago an old river rat named Ben was enjoying a day off on the beach with his girlfriend. They had been drinking and got a little carried away and well, a tour boat happened along about that time and- uh oh, Seering's waving me over. You're welcome to come tomorrow- bring your guitar. See you after dinner Schneids."

Schneider thought for a moment. When Kathy sidled up to the bar's waitress station to place a drink order, Schneider was ready; "Dan Seering has a pontoon boat and is taking it out tomorrow. Would you and your friends enjoy a river cruise?"

"Sounds great. Let me check with them and I'll let you know," Kathy said. "Can you get us back in time for work?"

"I think that's a safe bet, since the captain's the boss," Schneider responded.

This was great. *Of course they'd all come. They don't know us yet and thus would have to protect one another from us degenerates*, he reasoned. Now he had one more step to perform. Liz was just finishing up so Schneider walked up to the stage.

"Liz, how about mixing our rehearsal tomorrow with a river cruise? Seering and some friends are taking their pontoon boat out tomorrow and I just asked Kathy if you ladies might want to come along. We could throw some tunes at each other on the beach."

"It's OK with me if it's OK with Kathy and Tammy. See ya later."

Liz snapped her guitar case shut and headed for the dining room. Schneider silently congratulated himself. Talk about a boatload! He went upstairs to get his guitar. He opened in 30 minutes.

****

"And now, the end is near…"
-Paul Anka

It was shaping up to be a good night. Schneider was in strong voice, the crowd seemed to appreciate his stuff and he even knew the requests he was getting. Tomorrow he would spend the day on the water with babes and river rats. Life was good.

Around 10:30, Wright and Nemo took a table near the stage. Seering would join them later. As Schneider started an old country number requested by one of Chicago's Cadillac Commandos looking to be about a hundred, he noticed that Izod Enforcer was back at the bar nursing a Drambuie with his buddies.

"My Way," came his command, loud enough to be heard over Schneider's song.

Schneider continued the Eddy Arnold tune for the Cadillac Commando, who was jabbering away at his wife, oblivious to the number he had just requested.

"*My Way*." This time a little louder. Nervous laughter from the bar. Schneider looked at Pecsi and DeNiro, staring at him behind their double Drambuies. Then he caught a glance and a wink from Mike the bartender.

Schneider stopped the old Eddy Arnold song dead in its tracks, paused until a dime could be heard falling on the floor, and then launched into Frank Sinatra's anthem.

Nemo and Wright, sufficiently greased by now, joined him on the second chorus. By the third, Cadillac commando and half the lounge was singing along. At the bar, Schneider could see Izod Enforcer wagging his finger as if conducting. It was glorious stuff.

Schneider followed up with another Sinatra song and then took his first break. He sat down with Nemo and Wright. Within moments the cocktail waitress handed him a drink. "Compliments of the Mayor," she whispered.

****

Seering plunked himself down at the table, taking a break of his own.

"Jeez, Schneids, taking a break already? We'll lose half the crowd." It was Midnight.

"Seering, shut the fuck up." Schneider suddenly felt awash in moral authority. It empowered him. David Schneider- King of the Lounge Lizards!

He thought it best to thank the Mayor for the drink, so he stood up and walked over to the Mafiosi gathered at the bar.

"Thanks for the drink- I'm David Schneider," he said, extending his hand.

"Bernie Colsen. Glad to meet you." *The look* was still there but there was warmth in the firm handshake. "This is Bob Bleighman," said Colsen, turning to the bear of a man beside him. "Don't make him angry."

Up close, Schneider could see a twinkle in Bleighman's eye. They shook hands. "We were playing a little golf this afternoon, Schneideky- you play golf?" asked Bleighman. <u>Schneideky</u>? How many ways could you bastardize a guy's last name? "No," Schneider said, smiling.

"Then fuck you," said the Mayor. They all broke into hysterical laughter. Bleighman gave Schneider a playful slap on the back, which nearly launched him through the picture windows.

"Looks like a good start to the season," Schneider said, trying to make conversation. "A lot of tourists in town."

All conversation instantly ceased. Colsen looked at Schneider as if he had just triple bogeyed or something.

"Those aren't tourists," the Mayor said.

"No?"

"Those are *visitors*."

"Visitors?"

"Visitors, guests, Mr. Schneideky- and we *love* them."

"Yes, sir. I'll remember that. Thanks again for the drink."

"Plenty where that came from Schneideky. Oh- can you do one more number for me? 'Lucille'."

"Jesus, I *hate* that song," said Schneider, before thinking.

"Yeah, I thought you might," laughed Colsen before giving him *the look*.

"Mr. Mayor, I'd be happy to!"

"Schneideky, you're going to work out just fine- carry on!"

Before starting his final set, Schneider stopped at the table with Nemo, Wright and Seering.

"I've got some passengers for tomorrow guys," he announced.

"We're already overloaded as it is Schneids," said Seering. "Ryker's going and there may be others."

"I've got girls coming."

"Welcome aboard!" grinned Nemo.

"*Ahhaaaar!*" added Wright, doing his best pirate imitation.

"By the way Schneids," Seering said in a low voice. "I don't want to alarm you, but the fire marshal was in here today doing an inspection. The place checked out all right but they found some suspicious material in the tunnel." The *tunnel* was a basement level corridor leading from the kitchen to the back of the building. Deep in the bowels of the old Inn, it provided access for service and deliveries.

"They're checking it out, and it's probably nothing, but I thought you should know since you'll be sleeping here."

"What do you mean suspicious material- like arson or something?"

"Not necessarily," Seering reassured him. "Just some flammable stuff that isn't normally used here- as far as I know. They took it away and we'll try to find out how it got there. With this old place, who knows?"

Schneider nodded. The River Inn had been built in 1896 and had a storied history. It had housed lumberman and gamblers, fisherman and trappers, missionaries and prostitutes (though not at the same time it was thought). There were even rumors that Al Capone had used it as a weekend getaway, much like his fellow Chicagoans did today. There was nearly a hundred years of memories tucked away in this place. Anything was possible.

Schneider was still considering the possibilities as he stepped to the stage, strapped on his guitar and began to play *Lucille*.

<u>3</u>

"I love the child,
who steers this riverboat…"
-David Crosby

The next morning was warm and sunny. Diesel fumes punctuated the fresh air as empty tour boats idled past the River Inn; boats and river rats starting the day's dance.

The main docks downtown weren't large enough for the entire fleet, so after the last trip of the day- usually the hop back from the Indian Ceremonial at Stand Rock around 11:00 PM, the boats would scatter to various smaller piers along the riverfront for the night. They would then saunter downstream to their assigned stations in the morning like children coming downstairs to breakfast. First, it was over to the fuel docks near the River Inn to top off.

Then the boats pulling the first morning trips would head downstream and downtown to pick up their morning charges at the main docks. Those boats not scheduled until later in the day would stay at their piers, the crews performing light maintenance and other chores.

Meanwhile, the swing crews- those that were on standby should they be needed immediately-motored out to a suitable staging area- invariably Bare Ass Beach-where they could get either up-river to pick up strays or down river to load a new tour quickly. Next door to the River Inn, the Apollo steamboat was preparing to get underway as well, her boilers starting to vent a little steam as they got up to temperature. Her crew consisted of two characters: a classic old fart right out of Dixie, Frank Allison, and a younger, classic- old- fart- in training by the name of Joe Redmund.

Frank Allison knew every cubic inch of the boat's authentic steam engine as well as every cubic inch of the river. He knew how you got an 85-foot boat with a beam of 20 feet through the thirty-foot narrows at the *Elbow* without becoming a pile of toothpicks and scrap iron. He and Redmund treated the old Paddle wheeler like it was their very own; like a public endowment that only *they* could keep alive. Perhaps they were right.

The spot on the river in which the Apollo docks and the River Inn stood, being only a few hundred yards above the dam and the town's main docks, was one of the widest points on the upper Dells. The river took a lazy turn to the left here as it widened to a width of two football fields- including *Bare Ass Beach*- narrowing again just below the *Jaws* of *High Rock* and *Romance Cliff.* These were shear sandstone cliffs that stood like ten story- high sentinels beckoning visitors through them. Once on the other side, the river's main channel would mostly remain a narrow canyon trail until widening again into the Great Bay at *Stand Rock*.

The *Jaws* reminded Schneider of the Sirens' walls of *The Odyssey*. Maybe he should strap himself to the pontoons the first time through, he thought, as they were certainly beckoning *him*.

He inhaled deeply and savored the fresh river air and the view from his apartment's deck, which was actually the roof of the River Inn's lounge. He felt confident that he could be happy living in a cardboard box if it was sitting near the water.

Schneider preferred big water, the Great Lakes or the ocean, but would always remember what Seering had told him about rivers; *they were alive- constantly changing,*

*the waters always coming from somewhere
and always going somewhere. One day the
channel was here, the next day, there. And
this particular stretch of river could turn ugly
or beautiful in an instant- all by itself. It
didn't need any outside influences like the
weather or the seasons. It was petulant. It
gave no excuses.*

Schneider was a bit like that, he
mused, and he poured his last sip of black
coffee into the muddy water in tribute. He
looked up to see a hideously colored yellow
pontoon boat approaching the River Inn's
small pier.

"Mornin' Schneids," Seering called up
from the boat. "Kenny said it would be OK
to dock the boat here for the summer as long
as we leave enough room for his old Chris-
Craft. Get down here and help with these
lines."

"Kenny" was Ken Klinke, the River
Inn's second owner. Klinke also owned the
town's main supermarket and was the nicest
guy you'd ever want to meet. He had a
daughter, Debbie, and she and Seering dated
occasionally. Seering always dated more than
one girl at a time, however, and had

sometimes gotten himself into trouble because of it.

"Couldn't you have picked something a little flashier?" Schneider said sarcastically, looking at the boat. "My God, Seering, even the catfish'll be scared shitless."

"Yeah, but I got a great deal on it," responded Seering. "It's last year's model and it's never been used."

"I have no doubt about it," muttered Schneider as he put a half hitch around one of the pier's pilings.
"Hey smartass, you want to come or not?"

"Sure… has Wright seen the boat yet? I mean, he's actually got some taste and--"

"Wright's just as cheap as I am, asshole. He'll love it."

"Where is he?" asked Schneider.

"Camp Upham Woods- we're going to pick him up there." Camp Upham Woods, where Wright lived and worked, was situated on the river's old channel, near The *Elbow.*

If you were navigating the river and wanted to go upstream from the River Inn, you had two choices once you got past the *Jaws.*

You could go right, through the main channel and The *Elbow*, a ninety-degree turn through a thirty-foot wide narrow with sheer cliffs on either side. It carried swift currents and deep, deep water. Some locals swore it was three *hundred* feet deep here but no one really knew; soundings were impossible, and who would dive down to disprove it?

Or you could go left, around the other side of *Blackhawk Island* through an old quiet, shallow riverbed.

Both channels had their pleasures. One was serene and peaceful, the other eerie and breathtaking. There were times, however, when there was only one prudent course for the small private boat captain. Those times were 12:30 and 4:45. That was when the largest tour boat on the river, the *Clipper Winnebago* came through the Elbow.

The Clipper was 72 feet long with a beam of 22 feet, giving her between twelve and fifteen feet of clearance between her and the rocks at the crook of the Elbow. If she was in the center of the channel, that left 6 to 7 feet on either side. This would vary with the changing water levels and the season.

If you had a 6-foot wide boat and caught *The Clipper* coming through the middle of the elbow- you practiced a maneuver known by the locals as "climbing the walls."

Additionally, there was always a chance of meeting the *Apollo*, as her schedule varied depending on the whims of her crew and the available passengers. *Apollo* was just as big as the *Clipper*, but she was harder to maneuver, due to her great height and paddlewheel propulsion.

In any event, local knowledge was a valuable commodity on the Upper Dells of the Wisconsin River. Schneider giggled as he recalled the price of Seering's local knowledge of the Lower Dells years earlier. His giggle turned into a guffaw.

"What the hell are you laughing at Schneider?"

"Nothing. We're going to have some awfully pretty girls on board today, Seering. Try to keep your eyes on the road."

****

Dale Ryker walked out onto the pier with two shopping bags full of bratwurst, buns and chips. As he approached the gaudy little pontoon boat, he dropped the grocery bags and made a "cross" sign out of his two forefingers as if warding off evil.

"Whoa- that's bright!" he observed. Seering gave Schneider a side-ways glance. "I didn't tell you Schneids, Dale and I are roommates for the summer. Since the apartment has three bedrooms, Bob King wanted to take advantage of it- and us. He's putting one of his perennial pickers from The Showboat in there as well. Name's Joel Ireland. Plays banjo, guitar, mandolin, you name it. He bought into the boat and is coming today too."

In addition to co-owning the River Inn, Bob King owned a cash cow up on Broadway called *The Showboat*. It was a family place with a bar and a piano and banjo music and peanuts on the floor. Its nightly sing-a-longs was one of the town's mainstay attractions.

"Joel's bringing his guitar- why don't you get yours," ordered Seering.

"Aye, aye, sir," saluted Schneider as he greeted Ryker. By the time he returned Nemo had arrived and was loading a charcoal grill and a cooler on board.

Just then Joel Ireland appeared at the dock. Ireland could have just stepped out of *Gentleman's Quarterly*. Coifed blonde hair atop a pair of Ray-ban Wayfarers, Polo shirt,

Sportif shorts and Docksiders. Under his arm was a *Guild* guitar case. He gave the yellow pontoon boat a disparaging look and introduced himself to Schneider in a deep baritone.

A screech in the parking lot interrupted the introductions as a bright red GTO convertible came to a stop near the dock. Out jumped Kathy, Tammy and Liz, all in bikinis and T-shirts.

"Forget every nasty thing I ever said about you, Schneids," said Seering as they watched them approach. Kathy made the round of introductions and then they were ready to go.

"Nice boat, Dan," said Tammy, as they headed up river. "Was this the only color available?"

Ryker knelt down, dipped his hands in the river and splashed the boat's yellow sides, as if with holy water.

"*Von Scrotum the Third compels you!*" he chanted. Schneider merely glanced at Seering and chuckled.

"This boat needs a name," scowled Seering.

"How about '*The Yellow Menace*,'" shot back Tammy. Sassy. Big brown eyes. Schneider liked her immediately.

"One of your playmates isn't with us yet," said Kathy, pointing out the fact that the boat's fourth owner, Dave Wright was not yet aboard.

"Shouldn't you wait for him to discuss this?"

"Ahh, Wright'll go along with whatever we decide," said Nemo.

"I think we kids should decide this amongst ourselves," mocked Joel. "You know," he said, looking at Seering and Nemo, "we must be the oldest kids still in the Dells."

Soon they could see a wide sandy beach to port.

"Is that where we're going after we pick   up your friend?" asked Liz.

"Yes- that's Bare Ass Beach," announced Seering in his best tour-guide voice.

"How'd it get the name Bare Ass Beach?" asked Tammy, walking over to Seering at the steering wheel.

"Well," the tour-guide voice again, "back at the turn of the century, loggers would come through with their giant rafts of timber and would want to rest here. They would also take advantage of the quiet shallow water to bathe. One day the original Apollo comes steaming through and sees all these guys bare-ass naked washing on the beach. So the skipper of the Apollo nick-names the place Bare Ass Beach."

Schneider shot a questioning look over to Nemo but saw he was engrossed in conversation with Kathy.

Names of beaches and boats were still being discussed as they passed Blackhawk Island and entered the old riverbed. Schneider took out his guitar and approached Liz, who was sitting on the bow.

"Thought we might try a few possibilities," he suggested. As they tried out their first number, Schneider was struck by Liz's ability to pick up harmony lines as well as her sensitivity to the lyric. Schneider had always preferred ballads to up-tempo music. To him, a ballad was to music what a portrait was to painting.

Schneider had once read that van Gogh preferred painting portraits to painting grand cathedrals and other contemporary favorites *"for there is something in the eyes that is not in the cathedral."*

Schneider felt the same way about music. It appeared Liz did as well.

The boat slipped through the still water, Schneider and Liz sang together and all was right with the world.

When Wright came aboard at Camp Upham Woods, the conversation regarding a name for the boat switched into high gear.

"It should reflect our high standing in this community," quipped Wright. "After all, we are the oldest kids in the Dells.

"Oldest Kids in the Dells," nodded Ryker. He looked up, suddenly inspired. "O...K...I...T, no ...D."

"OKID" - said Joel. "We're a bunch of OKIDs!"

By this time the cooler of beer and wine was half-empty and everyone was getting a little goofy. The ugly yellow pontoon boat erupted into jingles and phrases containing the acronym *OKID*.

The party landed at Bare Ass Beach and the *Okid* Army went ashore with the *Okid* Grill and the *Okid* guitars and the now-official *Okid* volleyball net. Joel joined Liz and Schneider for some music and everyone played beach volleyball until it was time to head back for work.

Before disembarking at the River Inn dock, it was decided that a moonlight cruise after bar time was in order. All Okids should meet at the dock.

There were no dissenters.

****

"We are the people our parents warned us about..."
-J. Buffett

Around 2:00 AM that morning Okids started to gather down on the dock. Seering had invited Mike the bartender along, and between them they had managed to scrounge up a couple bottles of good champagne for the evening's cruise.

Joel showed up with a couple waitresses from the Showboat and Schneider's sister Debi had come up from Madison for the evening. Added to the regular cast of characters from that afternoon, there was quite a boatload preparing to board the yellow pontoon boat. Seering and Tammy were already on the boat, talking quietly near the stern.

As Schneider helped people aboard, he noticed the boat was getting lower and lower in the water. The moon was just coming up, but it cast enough light to indicate to Schneider that this was not a good situation. He called Seering over.

"Seering, I can't see the pontoons."

"Yeah, but it'll get brighter as the moon gets higher," Seering said, smiling aft at Tammy.

"That's not what I mean Seering- the pontoons are under the water. We've got too many passengers."

Seering looked at the pontoons, now completely submerged.

"Get in the boat Schneids."

"But the pontoons are under water."

"Get in the boat Schneids."

Schneider was not by nature a cautious person. Seering was. But at this moment Dan Seering appeared to be afflicted by that which will zap a life's worth of hard-earned good sense and foresight in the wink of an eye. Big brown ones, in this case. It was causing what columnist George Will once described as a *versatility of convictions.* Schneider pressed on.

"Seering, your boat appears to be sinking."

"Lighten up, Schneider. We're just going to Bare Ass. You coming or not?"

Schneider looked at Liz sitting on the bow with her guitar. He loosened the dock lines and threw them onto the boat, then followed them aboard. The rising moon was three-quarters full and waxing. It was hard to believe it would get better than this. Low on the horizon, it appeared to swallow the entire river, like a giant anti-black hole. Schneider pictured the headlines in tomorrow's paper:

UGLY YELLOW BOAT CAPSIZES OKIDS DIE DUE TO BIG BROWN EYES

At least they had enough life jackets on board. Seering had taken care of that before he had turned into a lunatic. Schneider wondered how long it would take for all of them to float down river and over the dam after the
boat sank.

It was a long, slow slog but they eventually pulled up to Bare Ass Beach.

"I have a question…"

Schneider froze. It was the voice from the speakers. The *hostess* was aboard! She sounded even sultrier without the amplification. Schneider's eyes followed the incredible tones to the starboard side and saw a figure silhouetted in the moonlight.

It matched the voice. Schneider couldn't make out the color of her hair but it hung to her waist and just over her butt, which looked to be right out of a Levi's ad. She was standing at the transom rail with Wright. She continued with her question.

"I've lived here all my life, but I still don't know how Bare Ass Beach got its name."

Wright took over this time. "Well you see Kerri, years ago when Frank Allison- do you know him? he pilots the Apollo - got married on the river. Actually had the ceremony done right on the Apollo. Anyway, it was a Saturday afternoon and this beach was packed with locals. As the Apollo went by, they all decided to give the happy couple a gift, so they mooned 'em. Every last local on the beach, bare-assed and bending over in the direction of the old steamboat. It was a beautiful thing." Wright sighed wistfully.

Schneider was incredulous. *Why was there always a boat going by?* Schneider considered the old adage about the tree falling in the woods and compared it to this bucket of bullshit. *No boats passing by, no Bare Ass Beach,* he concluded, and blamed the champagne for this riveting piece of pop philosophy- this revelation in the moonlight.

The hostess with the voice turned out to be Kerri Reasonor, a local beauty queen reputed to possess a huge libido, but very selective tastes.

Schneider's mind quickly went back to Liz and the music. They had three songs worked out now. By next weekend they'd be ready to share the stage for a half an hour or so. As they rehearsed their songs on the beach, champagne flowed into their glasses and people sang or danced along, swaying back and forth in the sand as the river flowed by in the moonlight.

It was around 4:30 AM when they swung into the docks at Camp Upham Woods to drop off Dave Wright. The moon was higher now and cast a pale yellow glow over the camp's riverfront, including the boathouse.

"What's in there?" asked Schneider.

"The canoes," answered Wright.

"Let's go for a canoe ride!" said Tammy. Wright resisted the rising cacophony until Kerri Reasonor's incredible voice could be heard from water. She had rolled up her tee shirt and had twisted the fabric to form a midriff. She was standing knee deep in the water, her cut-off shorts not yet wet.

"I love canoeing- let's race. Wright and I against y'all."

That did it. The canoes and the paddles and the PFDs flew out of the boathouse. Everyone paired up and climbed into the shiny aluminum canoes, ready to do battle. It was decided to race to the main channel and back, the first team to return to the boathouse would be crowned the winners.

The OKIDs proved to be a competitive group and somewhere between start and finish the race turned into a naval battle. Oars splashed and poked, canoes became torpedoes, and cries of "PREPARE TO BE RAMMED!" echoed up and down the old riverbed.

Soon this race-turned-naval battle evolved into a rescue and recovery operation as every boat but one eventually overturned in the shallow waters. Joyous cries of victory could be heard over the laughter as Dave Wright and Kerri Reasonor climbed the roof of the boathouse and sprayed the last bottle of champagne over themselves. Seering and Tammy came in a distant second.

By this time the camp's counselors, thinking that someone had broken into the boathouse, came out to investigate. The high school-aged counselors appeared a bit confused until seeing their supervisor on the roof of the boathouse, behaving like he had just won the America's Cup, shaking a bottle of champagne over a woman who looked like she had just won a wet T-shirt contest.

"Mr. Wright," giggled one of the counselors, "you're always telling us what a worth-while job this is—You've just convinced us."

****

Dawn was just breaking as the pontoon boat kissed the edge of the River Inn dock. In a few minutes the sun would rise over the river where the moon had been just hours before.

Sunday's were to become a special day at the River Inn, according to Seering and Ryker. They had decided that the dining room would host the town's most elaborate Sunday brunch. The menu would be extensive, the preparation time consuming. In fact, it was already getting too late to start. They would have to hurry if the crepes and tortes and mimosas were to be ready for the 9:00 am opening.

Schneider went straight to bed, remembering that next week he would start the alternating weekend janitor duties after bar time and dish washing duties during Sunday Brunch. This day, however, had been sublime.

Schneider fell into bed remembering champagne and music, moonlight and laughter, tall tales and small confessions.

As he drifted off to sleep a thought occurred to him, and he wondered how many of his friends, old and new, may have just fallen   in   love   tonight.

4.

"La Te Da"
-Van Morrison

The old lady on the swing smiled and gave a sigh as she watched the two young women run to the red convertible and turn out of the parking lot.

She had walked to the City Park out of lack of anything better to do. She had come to feed the birds and to feel sorry for herself. Finding the pigeons over by the swing set, she had sat down on the end swing and had reached into her pocket for some sunflower seeds.

Suddenly she was airborne and looked back to see two lovely girls smiling up at her. When she returned to the ground the one with the big brown eyes gave her a gentle shove and once again sent her spirit soaring. How wonderful the rushing air felt against her skin!

The young women introduced themselves as Tammy and Kathy. They talked for a while and then Tammy had told the old woman they had to go but would see her again another day and to be sure to keep coming to the park.

"The birds would miss you if you didn't," she smiled. Then they had sped off.

The old woman laughed and sighed again as she watched the red convertible head up Broadway towards River Road. How wonderful they had made her feel!

****

*"Listen to the rhythm
of the falling rain..."*
-J. Gummoe

Summer weekdays in the Dells were just like weekends without the cartoons. On a drizzly Thursday morning Schneider got out of bed and walked down to the dining room. A couple weeks had gone by and he was beginning to feel at home. He was looking forward to breakfast in the dining room followed by a good book overlooking the river. Mike was in the lounge doing inventory and taking pictures of wine bottles, so he went in to shoot the shit.

The *Cascades* were on the jukebox, singing in the rain. Two men were sitting at the bar. Older gentlemen, both in shirtsleeves and dungarees. On the bar in front of them were two half-full glasses of draft beer and two shot glasses. Both of *them* were empty. Schneider glanced at his watch. It was 9:50 AM.

The two men were simply sitting at the bar. No conversation, no movement- just sitting there as if spacemen in suspended animation. Schneider and Mike exchanged quips about the previous week's activities on the river and previewed the upcoming weekend. Another river outing was being planned.

Suddenly one of the old spacemen looked at Schneider and exclaimed "Junior! You sing!" He spoke with a jolly, Slavic accent of some sort. "You know *'She's too fat for me'*?"

The two men ordered another round, which consisted of two draft Heinekens and two shots of Stolichnaya. They introduced themselves as Stan and Fran.

Schneider squelched a giggle. Both were from Joliet and shared a factory gig outside of Chicago. Judging from the wad of bills Fran pulled out of his pocket to replenish the bar change, Schneider guessed they were long-time union. Neither wore wedding bands. Schneider glanced at the time again and wondered how many rounds that made so far.

"Junior, you like good Polish breakfast?" asked Fran, smiling with straight teeth through a crooked smile.

"Michael, get Junior here good Polish breakfast- like we have!" Stan was smiling too.

Mike pulled a frosted mug out of the bar's freezer, filled it with Heineken, then floated two raw eggs on top of the foam. He handed it to Schneider. Now they were all smiling. All but Schneider.

"Down you go Junior! This good for you- put meat on your bones!" cried Fran.

Stan leaned over as if he was confiding in Schneider and spoke softly. "You know what else this good for Junior?" He made a pumping motion with his fist, and the men howled with laughter.

Schneider stared at his 'breakfast'.

Being a singer had its uses. It was now or never. He willed his throat open and drained the glass in two large gulps. He could feel his cholesterol count soar as he resisted the urge to belch. Stan and Fran slapped him on the back and ordered him another one.

****

"*Take me where the wave and rock and tall pines meet…*"

- D. Seering

By Two O' Clock that afternoon the sun had chased the rain away and Schneider was reclining on the rooftop deck with a trashy novel in his hands. He had just retrieved some sunglasses and a pair of binoculars from his room when Seering climbed up from his apartment's porch to join him. He carried a six-pack of *St. Paulie Girl* beer and a clipboard. He paused to take in the bluffs and the huge white pines surrounding them.

"Schneids, go get your guitar. I wrote a poem here that I want to set to music." He handed it to Schneider. The poem told the story of a legendary Winnebago Indian leader named Yellow Thunder, who lived and died in the Dells area in the 1800s. Like other Native Americans, Yellow Thunder and his people had been forced from their traditional tribal lands by the Federal government, offering him a bribe, then "escorting" him and his people to reservations in the west.

Yellow Thunder went along quietly, urging his people to do the same. Many were confused, incensed, but they followed.

The solders returned in the spring with stories of incredible hardships endured in the frozen wastes to the west where the Winnebago were left behind. They were in for a surprise, however, because Yellow Thunder had beaten them back to Wisconsin and used their bribe to purchase a thousand choice acres on the river, where he stayed with his people until he died at age 100.

When it came his time to die, Chief Yellow Thunder requested that he be taken to the banks of the Wisconsin River "where wave and rock and tall pines meet" and to be faced west to meet his Maker.

Seering was a student of the area's history; he surrounded himself with original music, original art. All local. He thought Yellow Thunder's story especially poignant because he had overcome great odds and had done so without violence. Seering verbalized all this to Schneider, and by the time the last two beers were cracked, Schneider played back the song they had just written together.

They sat watching the river and the bluffs through whistling pine trees- the same ones that had probably stood as saplings at the time of Yellow Thunder's return. Then they tapped their beer bottles together in a toast and poured the remaining contents down into the swirling river. They sang their song to the river and the river sang back.

****

By this time it was 4:30 in the afternoon. *The Apollo* came into view, steaming down-river back to her dock next to the River Inn. This was Seering's call back to work, and he left Schneider on the Inn's rooftop to marvel at the old paddle wheeler.

She was not like the noisy steel hulled, diesel gulping stinkpots that made up the

DBC fleet. Like the river, *Apollo* was somehow alive. She breathed, she sang, she creaked in her old age. She was beautiful.

As she continued her promenade down river, her steam whistle blew and Schneider could begin to hear the cascade of water falling off her stern, guiding her home.

Looking between her whitewashed wooden beams, Schneider could see that this had been another light day for Allison and Redmund; only a handful of passengers could be seen on board. *The Apollo* rarely carried a full complement of passengers like the other tour boats did. *Apollo*'s owners didn't have the cash flow and the resources that Dells' Boat Company did. They couldn't afford a ticket stand on every corner of town. They couldn't hire swarms of kids to peddle rides. They couldn't sponsor spots on the local radio station every eighteen and a half minutes. And *Apollo*'s docks weren't on Broadway, with its high traffic and high visibility.

When a crowded DBC tour boat passed her directly off the River Inn, however, Schneider could see *every* camera come out to take photos of the lovely vessel. It punctuated the growing disdain that

Schneider, though he was young, had harbored about the times he was living in. Nothing illustrated the rationale for his attitude better than what he was now seeing; something noble and beautiful being simply observed, then discarded by people who were unable or unwilling to get off the beaten path. Those folks would probably get off the DBC boat on Broadway, drive through the Burger King on their way back to the Holiday Inn, get their one-hour photos developed, and actually think they had experienced something. Fast food and fast thrills. Follow the billboards. Lives of convenience.

Ignorance was bliss, but Schneider suddenly felt sorry for those on the DBC boat who would be content with a snapshot of the Apollo and not the experience of being aboard her.

At the same time, he couldn't understand the bitterness he felt over such a seemingly trivial observation. He once again found himself immersed in a familiar stream of consciousness.

Perhaps it had something to do with losing his mother at such a young age. Back then he couldn't understand why he was the only kid in the neighborhood having to go home after school without his mother to greet him at the door. Sometimes during lunchtime, he would slip out of school, head home, and secretly pass the time alone, listening to his Dad's or Debi's records while his classmates ate and went to recess.

He would sing along to the records, picturing himself as a crooner in the movies. He repeated the process after school while looking out the living room window, waiting for his father's car to appear in the driveway. His father married a fine woman several years later, but Schneider had always kept a picture of his mother with him.

A photo without the experience.

He had always felt different than the others, just as he did at this moment. Actually, for various reasons, half the kids in America were now growing up like he did, he realized. He shook his head, trying to shake himself loose of his angst.

He really had no reason to be so irascible. He was having a wonderful time this summer; his wanderlust being quenched in this town of rednecks and poets. Why did he always dwell on the negatives rather than the positives? Why couldn't he be more like Seering? Seering seemed reflective, even introspective at times, but unlike Schneider he was always optimistic. Seering simply concentrated on the up-side.

Schneider got up and started towards the lounge. As he did so, he remembered an interview he had once read with his favorite actor, who had confided *"I need my anger- it keeps me sharp, makes me function- it's my toolbox."*

It occurred to Schneider at that moment, for the first time in his life, that this brooding side of himself was perhaps essential to whatever talent he possessed. He envisioned the Lady of the Scales and hoped that the positive aspects of this- *trait* within him would outweigh and outlast the negatives. He was nothing if he was not creative. He understood then, why so many celebrities and artists seemed to live such screwed up lives.

He also understood at that moment that the *same* traits that give rise to an individual's strengths also lead inevitably to their weaknesses.

Generations before his seemed to accept this instinctively. Perhaps that is why men and women used to stay together. They kept families together and intact. It was a physical law- like $E=mc^2$. You ignored it at your own peril. Not so anymore, and Schneider feared the implications.

He shrugged this off and watched as Frank Allison guided the Apollo alongside the dock without so much as a tap, and Redmund stepped out to secure her lines.

****

Webster defines the word *Dell* as "a small deep valley; a hollow." The name is derived from the French word *Dalles,* meaning "slab-like rock." Both derivatives are aptly descriptive.

Wisconsin Dells has been unique for 500 million years. That's when some of the purest quartz on the planet, whipped up by intense winds at the end of the Cambrian period, formed monstrous deposits of white sandstone. Geologist Paul Herr describes the resulting formations as colossal "fossilized sand dunes."

Much later, as the last ice age was ending 15,000 years ago, a mammoth glacier carved its way southeast on a collision course with these formations, then suddenly stopped less than four miles away. As the glacier melted into the huge craters it had dug on its journey, forming lakes, the remaining ice of its leading edge acted like a gargantuan dam, preventing a flood of almost biblical proportions.

Finally the ice wall gave way and sent a torrent of melt water into the quartz sandstone formations of the present day Dells. The resulting erosion carved the spectacular formations for which the area is known today. In fact, the river and the rain continue to carve the rocks to this day and what was once pure white sandstone continues to redden, as it is stained with iron from the hard Wisconsin waters.

These resulting sandstone behemoths that tower above the bottom of the river will always command the greatest respect from the river pilots whom, like Frank Allison, earn their living by negotiating with history.

****

"Gin and Ice, half from gone..."
- D. Seering

Schneider gingerly walked down the stairs to the lounge with his guitar- this time without incident. He was finally getting used to those damned steps. He had hopes of catching Liz before she started her first set. Maybe they could iron out a couple of rough spots in their latest duet. Liz wasn't there, but the crew of the Apollo II was, Redmund pulling on a beer and Allison sipping a shot of *Jack Daniels*. Mike was still behind the bar.

"Hey, Mike," said Schneider as he sat down at the bar.

"Back for another helping of beer and eggs?"

"Very funny. Hey, maybe Stan and Fran were right- maybe a diet of that stuff could put a couple of pounds on me," shot back Schneider, perpetually aware of his slight build. "Those guys were something else, he said. Are they staying here, at the hotel? Are they regulars?"

"Stan and Fran? Are you kidding? They're as regular as it gets. A week in mid-June and a week in late August. Been coming up for as long as I can remember."

Schneider shook his head. "Nine-thirty in the morning's a little early for beers chasing that Russian rocket fuel isn't it? What's the story?"

Mike had expected Schneider's question. He smiled and wiped the bar.

"Same drill every summer. They check in Saturday morning around nine. By 9:30 they're working on their first boilermakers. Around one they head in to the restaurant for lunch, then up to their rooms for a nap. Then it's out for some bumming, and by five O' Clock they're back in those seats for cocktails and dinner. Same schedule every day 'til checkout. I'm surprised you haven't noticed them."

"I'm surprised they're not dead," Schneider grimaced and thought for a moment. "Holy shit, how do they survive? How much do you figure they drop in a week?"

"I can tell you this much," mused Mike, "it affects my inventory- but they're well behaved, never seem drunk, no problems, and they tip well. They're good guys."

"I wonder if the *Guinness Book of World Records* knows about them?" Schneider pondered out loud.

"That's a thought- Have you met the guys from the Apollo?" asked Mike, motioning to them. Schneider turned towards them and extended his hand.

"David Schneider." He shook hands with Frank Allison and Joe Redmund. They were dressed in their uniforms of the day- white New Orleans-style shirts with red armbands, black slacks, and patent leather shoes.

Redmund was young, although he was approaching river rat status, after nine years on the river. He had started by selling tickets for DBC in high school, then drove a *"park and ride"* bus before becoming a guide and later a Captain on one of the DBC boats. This would be his third summer as First Mate on the Apollo, and it appeared as if he had found a home.

There was something oddly contemplative about Redmund, thought Schneider. His eyes had that *river rat* sparkle, but they betrayed forlornness. Even without the Dixieland get-up, Redmund seemed somehow out of place in this century. He wore his mustache waxed and turned up, and spoke slowly, deliberately, as if making sure each word was appropriate before adding it to the conversation.

Allison was different. He was older, having spent many years on the Mississippi piloting a majority of its large riverboats. Slight of build but clearly not a guy to be messed with, he possessed the highest rated masters' license on the river.

As they sat at the bar, Allison explained that he was semi- retired now, a widower with a daughter and grandchild living in nearby La Crosse.

"I'm just hanging around long enough to make sure Joe here has things under control, then I'll hang up my armband for good," he said. Schneider recalled the precision, no- the *grace* with which Allison had docked the proud old steamboat earlier that afternoon. It had been a *performance*- you didn't give a performance like that without experiencing a crystalline pure, sheer joy in what you were doing.

Sure you will, thought Schneider.

"Frank and I saw y'all on the pontoon boat last weekend" smiled Redmund. "Quite a-- boatload."

"You noticed that huh?" laughed Schneider.

"Pretty girls love boats," offered Allison, and he lifted his shot glass and continued to pontificate; *"She loved to contemplate her most transparent devices as marvels of low cunning..."*

Schneider recognized the passage from *Tom Sawyer*. The men raised their glasses just as Stan and Fran came in to reclaim their seats for the PM shift.

****

Tammy walked up to the pay phone near the lounge's coat rack and dialed the number from memory.

"Hi Mom, it's me...its going fine- in fact, it's going great...um hmm, the Manager is a great guy and he and his friends have a boat. We've been spending a lot of time on it. The river is beautiful here- pardon? Yeah, work is going fine too. Dan- he's the manager- is a really great guy. Oh- I wanted to find out about Ken- is he OK? Great. I'll send him a card but give him my love in the meantime. How's Suzie and Eric... Did they get my gift? Good. When can you come up- I miss you all and I'd like you to meet my new friends... OK, let me know. Kathy says hi by the way. Gotta go Mom, my shift is starting. I love you."

****

"Some say love, it is a river
that drowns a tender reed…"
- A. McBroom

Friday's late dinner crowd had replaced the cocktail crowd when Liz nodded at Schneider and smiled. It was 8:45. They would do a short set together before Schneider went on at 9:00.

Keeping in mind the demographics of the place, they started with a slow swing version of *Hey Good Lookin'*, which Liz had suggested the previous weekend. Schneider had almost ended the collaboration right then and there. But she had turned out to be right.

The combination of Liz' voice, her appearance, and the slower swing beat turned the venerable Hank Williams country classic into a steamy little number that left the bar's male patrons (and Schneider) somewhat short of breath.

Then came two love songs done as duets and another real oldie, *Sentimental Journey*, which prompted a nice old fart at the bar to yell "why aren't you kids on television?!"

Another nice, well-meaning rocket scientist, thought Schneider. The River Inn attracted a lot of silver-haired folks, which was where the money was, and it was becoming apparent to Schneider that those folks liked hearing "*their music*" done by "*fine young people.*" Maybe he and Liz were on to something. Besides, he sincerely enjoyed a lot of music from that era, having grown up with so much of his mother and father's music.

They closed with Liz singing *The Rose.* By the time they finished, Schneider would have jumped off *High Rock* if he thought it would help him get close to this woman, but so far Liz had left no hints that she was interested. In fact, she offered no information at all about her love life. There had been no boyfriends down to visit, no barroom romances, nothing.

A girl like that has __got__ to have them lined up around the block and hip deep. Schneider vowed to learn more about her. Maybe a woman like Liz would find it *difficult* to meet men simply because she was so intimidating, so- *perfect*, Schneider postulated. *Yeah, sure.*

Indeed, though it was becoming obvious that Tammy had seriously captured Seering's heart, Seering had leaned over to Schneider last weekend as Liz was walking out of the water at Bare Ass Beach. She had worn a black bikini that had set off her dark hair and thin hourglass figure. As she threw her hair back, water dripping off that flawless skin Seering had observed, quite clinically, that "she's a ten."

And in every sense, she was. Smart, talented, creative, confident and unbelievably pretty. Schneider knew he didn't stand a chance, but he was sure as hell going to try.

Liz took her bows and left the stage to Schneider.

It is absolutely astounding thought Schneider; *how many beautiful girls work in this place.*

To him though, Liz was becoming all he could see. He suddenly felt lonely without her. *Schneider, you are heading for a world of hurt,* he told himself, knowing he was powerless to stop it. At that moment he *could* have been stepping off a cliff. He was certain it felt the same.

"You have a request." The cocktail waitress interrupted his thoughts. She put a tonic and lime down on a bar napkin next to him, then smiled and returned to the service bar. Schneider picked up the drink and saw writing on the bar napkin. He sipped his drink and read

Play me a love song.
A secret admirer

Schneider looked around. The only women presently in the lounge were over fifty. *It could be one of the staff, or someone out on the deck. Maybe it's just a horny senior citizen.* He chuckled and played *Misty* for her, whoever she was.

Before he had finished, Stan and Fran had sat down at the bar after finishing their dinner and Bernie Colsen had wandered in with Bob Bleighman and the rest of the Friday Foursome. Schneider could see the frosty mugs and shot glasses come out for Stan and Fran, and snifters for the Foursome.

Schneider immediately began *My Way* and earned a Glenlivet on the rocks from the Mayor. Mike knew Schneider preferred non-alcoholic until Midnight, being well acquainted with the lounge lizards' main occupational hazard. Perhaps the Mayor had insisted.

As he finished the set, he saw Dave Wright pulling up a barstool.

"Evening Dave."

"Hey, Schneidy."

"Any fallout from Saturday's regatta?"

"No, and I don't seem to be getting as much shit from the counselors any more- especially the boys."

"I should say not- that was quite an inspiring image that Kerri- I mean you- burned into their minds that night."

"You were right the first time, Schneidy." Wright laughed. He looked at his drink.

"I'm having dinner with her tonight after her shift ends." Schneider thought about Kerri Reasonor. Like Liz, she was undeniably beautiful, but that was where the similarity ended. If Liz was a Mercedes, then Kerri was a Lamborghini- at Le Mans.

And Dave Wright was a Volvo. His was a most interesting and dangerous combination of virtues. He was good-looking so he naturally attracted attention. He was highly intelligent, even analytical, which led to much introspection. And he was extremely sensitive and spiritual. That could be an explosive mix where love was concerned.

If you could simply have some laughs and enjoy the carnal knowledge of a woman like Kerri, great. But guys like Wright and Schneider had a weakness for free spirits and found that hard to do without falling in love.

Schneider knew it was none of his business but he dove in anyway. "Having a woman like that could get you into some serious trouble. I mean no offense Dave, but I have nothing to do while singing on my barstool except hone my powers of observation. Every time Kerri walks through this bar _every_ head in the room turns. The men to admire her, the women to despise her. Did you notice the attention she was getting at Bare Ass? If I were you, I'd carry a baseball bat to dinner just in case."

Wright laughed again. "Schneidy, there's something about her…"

"Oh, I hear that. Well, we love what we love…" Schneider reflected, thinking again of something van Gogh had once said. "Now _you_ stay out of trouble."

Schneider squeezed Wright's shoulder and walked over to the cocktail waitress.

"Where did the note come from?" he asked.

"I wish I could tell you," she said. "Mike gave it to me." Schneider turned to Mike. "Well?"

"I'll never tell. But she went in to the dining room about an hour ago," said Mike with a wink. Schneider walked out to the dining room. It was thinning out now. Plenty of time for whoever had wrote the note to finish dinner. Schneider sighed, then smiled inwardly. He had never "had much game" where females were concerned. Maybe the singing would turn things around.

As he turned to head back out to the lounge, he saw Seering and Ryker speaking with a guy in a municipal uniform of some sort. He walked over.

"It's used as a solvent, and it's extremely flammable," the guy in the uniform was explaining. "You gotta have a license to use it. Have you hired any industrial cleaning crews or anything like that recently?"

"No," said Seering, "but I'll check with the owners."

"We already did," said the uniform, a deadly serious look on his face now. "Nothing."

Schneider looked closer and saw the badge of a city Fire Inspector.

"What would set it off?" asked Ryker. "I mean, it gets awfully hot in that kitchen sometimes."

"A good point," the fire inspector said. Relatively low ambient temperatures can bring that stuff to flashpoint, although it would have to be out of the can, you know, in a puddle or on a rag or something. The vapors are what you have to worry about. In most instances though, a spark or flame would be needed."

"So how *did* it get here?" asked Seering, looking at Ryker, then noticing Schneider standing there.

"I've heard rumors- that this place is for sale," the Fire Inspector went on haltingly. "I know for a fact what it takes to run a place like this and"--

"What are you saying?" interrupted Seering, his voice low now.

"I'm not *officially* saying anything, Mr. Seering. Just keep your heads up. I'll be in touch. By the way, the prime rib was excellent tonight."

The Fire Inspector walked away and joined a group of friends heading out to the deck.

"You didn't hear that," said Seering, turning towards his head chef and his entertainer before climbing the stairs to the office.

****

Randy Highridge watched the beach widen with the rising sun; long shadows being cast down its length as the sun cleared High Rock. It stained the surrounding cliffs a blood red and reflected off the green specks of tannic acid floating in the descending water. From a distance the beach appeared white, its water a deep blue.

When you were up close however, especially during these early morning hours, it was quite different, resembling a primordial awakening of sorts.

The formal ceremonial grounds of Stand Rock, up river in the Great Bay, was majestic and was revered by his people, the land which Yellow Thunder had acquired a century ago, but Randy had always preferred this spot.   The Highridges were prominent members of the Winnebago community and Randy's grandmother had acquired an imposing reputation for advocating a different brand of activism than their legendary Chief had demonstrated years ago. It had nearly landed her in jail on several occasions. Now she was an officer in the local Chamber of Commerce.

Randy reflected on this as he walked along the beach. You could easily wade in the river here due to the beach's gentle slope, which was an oddity on the *Dells*. Highridge's ancestors had used this beach as a place of meditation, a place to seek guidance from Earthmaker and to give thanks for good fortune. It had served as a place of rest and contemplation among the spires of stone and fast water.

Now Randy Highridge walked its length alone, enjoying the solitude. He knew it wouldn't last.

****

Schneider watched the lone figure stroll Bare Ass Beach from the windows of the River Inn's dining room. It was a Friday morning and Schneider was enjoying a cup of coffee before heading back to the kitchen and the dishwasher. He had agreed to fill in for the regular AM dishwasher, who had asked for the day off. June was history and Schneider had settled into the alternating weekend dishwasher routine per his agreement with Seering, but he was not enjoying it.

It made him realize, however, just how lucky he was to be able to sing for a paycheck. Maybe that had been part of Seering's strategy- to keep him from outgrowing his young britches. Indeed, it allowed him to see that in addition to temporary help like Schneider and Tammy and Kathy, there were some real pros that worked here as well. The River Inn Dining Room had been a popular venue for many years, and it enjoyed a highly competent core of bar staff and waitresses that returned season after season. In this regard the Dells' hospitality industry was much like the tour boats, combining *perennial* experience with an *annual* infusion of young enthusiasm. Seering had done a good job of balancing his wait staff between young, attractive students and older, experienced ladies and men.

There was much more to running a

place like this than Schneider had first thought.

His gaze shifted to the yellow pontoon boat resting at the dock, and Schneider fixated on the newly applied black letters on her side and stern:

OKID

"Mind if I join you?"

Schneider looked up and saw his father standing there, a newspaper folded under his arm.

"Dad!" Sit down, how are you doing?"

"Well, I had an appointment nearby, so I stopped in to ask you the same thing."

"It's been great so far, although Seering's got me doing dishes today."

"Good for him."

Schneider introduced his father to Kathy, who was working the breakfast shift, and asked for some more coffee.

"Stay for breakfast, Dad?"

"No, I've got to run. Actually we'll be coming for dinner tomorrow night with Dan's folks. I understand he's done a pretty good job with the kitchen."

"Yeah, he has. Try the Prime Rib. I imagine the Judge will want the Duck. I'll warn Seering that his father is coming so he can make sure it's well done."

"We'll come early so we have plenty of time to check out the entertainment afterwards," his father said with a smile.

"Turns out I'm not the only one playing here this summer," Schneider told his father. "There is a girl playing before me and wait 'til you hear her. We're doing some stuff together as well."

"Sounds great- we'll be looking forward to it. Clare sends her best by the way." The elder Schneider shifted in his seat. "Listen son, I wanted to tell you how proud I am of you keeping up your grades through all this, along with starting next semester at the University and all. I... just wanted to tell you that."

Schneider knew what his father was really saying; that he missed having him around the house. That after eighteen years it seemed unfair to be detached so suddenly. Schneider knew this because he felt the same.

His father had probably driven thirty miles out of his way to come here, no matter what he had said about a local appointment. At that moment Schneider wanted to hug his father and go home. He settled for a handshake.

"See you tomorrow then, Pop. I better be getting back to the kitchen."

****

"We've seen the light and lord, ain't it yellow…"
-D. Schneider

The next morning was once again spent provisioning the *OKID* for a day on the river. It was Saturday, July Fourth, and the staff would have to be back early. Things were already getting hectic. Ken Klinke's Chris Craft was available to act as a chase boat if Seering was needed right away. All other OKIDs settled in for a holiday weekend on the water.

Schneider was looking forward to having his Father, his Stepmother, and the Seerings at the River Inn that evening. If it weren't for the janitor duty that he was scheduled for after bar time, things would be perfect. He reminded himself to imbibe with moderation during what would be a long, long day. He had brought his guitar as usual so he and Liz could practice a bit.

The *OKID* landed at Bare Ass Beach and by late morning, chicken was roasting on the grill, the keg of beer was tapped and the usual volleyball game was proceeding.

Randy Highridge was there and had been joined by some friends, mostly dancers from the Indian Ceremonial. They had all joined the volleyball game. The beach was filling up quickly, and room was getting scarce.

Randy teased Seering about the Winnebago 'being there first' and how the *pinkos*, as he called the OKIDs, couldn't play a decent game of volleyball to "save their skins".

"A little 'Indian humor'," he added with a smile.

"All right, Randolph," said Seering, attempting to puff out his chest, which was difficult since he didn't have one, "it is obvious that this beach is too small for us white fo—

"White folks? Man, you said it," interrupted Highridge. "I've never seen such a collection of pale asses in my-

"As I was saying," continued Seering, trying to sound serious, "this beach is getting too small for the white man and the Winnebago."

"Actually", said Randy under his breath, "if the tourists would just get the hell out of here, we'd be all-- what do you suggest?"

"A regulation volleyball match. *Winnebago's* against the *Pinkos*- er, the Okids. Winners get The Beach."

After much verbal jousting it was agreed that on the following Sunday, beach volleyball history would be made- with squatting rights to Bare Ass Beach hanging in the balance.

After all the hoopla abated, Schneider looked over towards Liz. She had picked up his guitar and was singing with Joel and Wright, who had put together a contraption of some sort, and which Wright was now plunking at with reckless abandon.

"Schneidy, how do like my washtub bass?" said Wright as Schneider approached.

"Schneids you gotta hear this," said Joel. They played and Schneider listened.

"I never knew you played bass Dave. In fact, I never knew you were musically inclined at all," said Schneider.

"I don't and I'm not," answered Wright. "I just put this together 'cause I thought it might be fun."

"Sounds great to me," said Joel. "Tell you what- why don't you bring that thing up to the Showboat tonight and then we'll go back to the River Inn later and join Schneids?"

"Works for me," said Schneider, and Liz agreed to hang around after her set and join in as well.

****

That afternoon, on the way back down river, Schneider looked around him for the umpteenth time. There was something truly magical taking shape at this time, in this place, with these people.

He grabbed a pencil and paper and by the time the *OKID* got back to the dock everyone aboard was singing along to a new tune:

Start spreading the word gotta shout, gotta bellow
We've seen the light and Lord ain't it yellow
And it lights up the way to good friends old and new
You got your Wrights, got your Nemos got your Seerings too
Before too long we'll have all of Timbuktu
Riding down the river on a boat called the you-know-who
OKID yellow, everybody singing hello...

<u>5</u>

"Somebody come and save me from this madness..."
- Dan Hicks and his Hot Licks

Schneider laughed out loud and the reverberations startled him as he put away the vacuum cleaner. Bathrooms were next. The silence enveloping the River Inn was oppressive.

It was 3:00 AM and the Fourth of July was officially over. It had been a great day on the river and the evening had also gone well. Schneider's folks had come up for dinner as promised and had met the Seerings at the River Inn. David and Dan both were able to join them.

Both sons enjoyed their parents' company enormously and especially liked getting both families together. The elder Schneider/Seering combination had been responsible for more than a few great parties that both David and Dan remembered. Prime rib and duck and shrimp were served and good conversation ensued, including some old Navy stories.

After dinner Schneider introduced his father and stepmother, as well as the Seerings to Mayor Colsen and all the OKIDs. Then they all serenaded the lounge with some old campfire music from Lake Eleanor. Wright and Joel showed up as promised and sat in for the final set, and Liz, Kathy and Tammy stuck around as well. The music had flowed, the bar did well and everyone was happy.

Now, in the course of one hour, Schneider had been transformed from Ringmaster to the *Guy Cleaning the Toilets*.

His laughter echoed through the darkened empty rooms, sending a shiver up his spine. He rechecked the doors leading from the river and the deck, and entered *the tunnel*, which lead to the cleaning supplies and the rear rest rooms.

Upstairs, Seering and Ryker would be rising in another hour and a half to come downstairs and start preparations for Sunday Brunch. Schneider hoped to be in bed by then.

He couldn't stop thinking about what the Fire Inspector had said the night before. He hadn't heard a word about Klinke or King wanting to sell the place. Walking through the tunnel, though, it was easy to see why as businessmen they might need to try.

The River Inn was a grand old building and it required constant upkeep and a steady infusion of money just to keep it standing. Just last week water had backed up in the game room during a storm. Schneider would never forget seeing Seering knee-deep in sewage at six in the morning with a mop in one hand and a telephone in the other trying to get things cleaned up before the breakfast shift began. Seering had mentioned a new roof would be needed before winter and the air conditioning was way overdue for an overhaul.

Of course, the River Inn was a wooden structure on a river and was over 80 years old. The insurance on it had to be astronomical. If the owners were trying to sell and couldn't, having the place burn to the ground could make certain problems go away. As he wheeled the cleaning cart out of the tunnel and into the back hall towards the restrooms, he thought he heard something and froze. He listened for a while but heard nothing further except the whine of the AC. Maybe there was late night activity in the game room out by the pool. He took two more steps and heard it again.

There is definitely someone else in this building down here and close by. Now he waited again.

Silence.

I'm turning into a paranoid old lady. Afraid of my own shadow, he scolded himself. If he didn't get his ass in gear soon, he'd never get any sleep. He finished up the bathrooms and walked upstairs to his room, trying to shake the feeling that there had indeed been someone downstairs close by in the tunnel.

****

There are certain places on Earth- tourist towns mostly- that seem to produce per capita far more than their share of notable characters and occurrences. These locations often produce a disproportionate body of great literature, great art and, it should follow, pertinent thinking- all produced by singular characters. What is the formula, the calculus that makes this so?

Dave Wright pondered this question while once again waiting for Kerri to get off work at his regular spot next to the River Inn bar's waitress station. He concluded that there were two main contributing factors resulting in such places:

The first was a preponderance of water.

The second was the preclusion of "steady work."

The combination of these two forces sets in motion the evolution of a *tourist town*. It is cyclical and happens something like this: A picturesque place on an ocean or a lake or a river attracts a few dreamers willing to simply sit and contemplate the view.

Next, adventurers and other people of spirit, attracted by the view and by the dreamers, come to live. They eke out a living, and certain entrepreneurs emerge to thrive while serving these pioneers. Everyone enjoys themselves- thus the *golden years*.

Before too long, word spreads and wealthy people begin to arrive. They come to enjoy the lifestyles of the original dreamers, but bring along much more cash, and a lot of spare time in which to spend it. This in turn supports the entrepreneurs.

This leads to another influx of dreamers, content to serve and entertain the entrepreneurs and the well healed loiterers of means. They bend to this servitude because they basically have a hell of a good time between shifts. This marks the tourist town's *mature phase.*

Occasionally, regardless of phase, the particularly talented amongst these throngs of dreamers and peasants are able to produce some truly enlightened, perspicacious works. How long a tourist town stays in this productive, creative epoch before succumbing completely to its growing wealth and turning into one enormous Hilton Hotel remains a measure of its character. The life cycle of such a tourist town can be plotted on a graph. Time on the horizontal axis, average disposable income on the vertical. The graph's middle area represents the creative era. If Wright had to plot Wisconsin Dells on such a continuum, he would do so at the halfway point of an increasingly steep curve.

Asked to support this thesis, he would proffer numerous individuals that helped create the Dell's legend. He thought about some of them while Mike refreshed his drink. There was of course H.H. Bennett, artist and photographer, whose images of the rafters and the river attracted the town's early dreamers.

But never mind the *Historical Society*-types. Some of Wright's contemporaries, names like Fudd Foss, Honker John, Chief Nightsun, and Sly Phil the Evil Dr. Fernornten would forever be on the lips of even the casual student of Dells history. Presently Wright considered each while tinkling the ice in his glass with his forefinger.

Fred "Fudd" Foss had been a Duck Driver extraordinaire. He once hosted a 'Washington crosses the Delaware' party. Foss was George Washington and the lower Dells of the Wisconsin River was The Delaware River. The crossing was accomplished in a Duck with coworkers all dressed up in Revolutionary War garb. Of course, this had to be done at midnight. Unfortunately, some of the area's residents complained to the police about the noise caused by the Ducks diesel engines and the crossing was aborted- well, busted. Some people just had no reverence for history. Wright stirred his drink.

Chief Nightsun was the last of the old school of real Indian guides on the Lower

Dells. The chief had lost both arms at an early age in a sawmill accident. On the boat tours he gave a beautiful talk about his people, the Winnebago. Now, the main income of the river guides was derived from selling guidebooks that were handed out at the beginning of the tour. On the way back to the docks, the guide or captain would explain that passengers could hand the books back in to the guide or keep them for a "nominal fee." The problem was, Nightsun didn't have any hands in which to take back the guidebooks. Reflecting on this, Wright couldn't remember whether that had helped him or hurt him. Wright ordered another drink.

Honker John was a mentor to both Wright and Seering. He was a tall, dark-skinned guy with a very large stomach. Honker had worked the lower Dells for years and knew every possible trick to take money out of the tourist's wallet. He had been tasked with teaching his young charges all the names of the river's various rock formations like "Baby Grand Piano" and "The Hawks Bill." There was one rock formation that was supposed to look like a rabbit. One day Wright had canoed up to it and found that the rabbit's tail had been *painted* on. However, when viewed from a particular prescribed angle and distance, you couldn't tell.

Seering and Wright did some investigating and found that Honker John had been behind the enhancement. They were scheduled to go out on an actual tour with Honker the next morning to see his presentation first hand and had decided to do some *enhancing* of their own. They took Dan's runabout out to another famous rock formation called "Rafter's Hook," which resembled a lumberman holding a long hook used in snaring the old rafts of lumber and securing them to shore. The *hook* was a genuine iron rod from that era which had remained anchored in the sandstone.

Seering and Wright bent the tip of the rod upwards and motored over to the prescribed viewing location in which the tour boat guide would explain the formation to the boat's passengers. They looked back toward the formation. That now appeared to be one *happy* lumberman. The next day they took great pleasure in observing Honker John ad-libbing his way through a most interesting segment of the tour. It was immediately dubbed "Honker's Hook."

While Wright and Seering had been undergoing their indoctrination down on the lower Dells with Honker John, Nemo had spent his time up on Broadway being trained in the fine art of ticket selling by Sly Phil, the Evil Dr. Fernornten. The Doctor was of medium height, had striking white hair, rosy cheeks and a protruding belly. He was famous for his wonderful wit, loud endless chuckle, and his ribald poetry. He was an ardent collector of skin magazines and sexual aids. Every morning before work began, Dr. Fernornten would show young Nemo a new sexual device and explain its use. After work, Sly Phil would make his regular rounds of the town's taverns. He told Nemo to avoid him after 5:00 pm because he would "very likely be in a melancholy state. He died shortly thereafter but gave his favorite student a poem to remember him by:

■■

When I am old and in my grave
No more women will I crave
But on my tombstone I want written
I've had my fill, and I'm not shittin'

And also upon it I'd like wrote
Many a drink has gone down my throat
So if someday, my grave
* you should pass by*
Just piss on me 'cause
I'm always dry.

Thank you... thank you very kindly!

By the time Wright's third drink came around, he was in a highly nostalgic mood. He and Mike compared old war stories about obtaining their captain's licenses. It was agreed that Seering's saga had been the best.

To get a U.S. Coast Guard 60-ton license, the minimum required to pilot a boat for hire on the Wisconsin River, you had to pass a very difficult exam. One of the prerequisites for taking the exam was to have 100 hours of experience piloting a boat under a licensed captain. At the time, Seering had been on a tour boat less than a handful times in his life and had never paid the least attention about how to drive them. He inquired as to how he would get his experience and was told to report to the *White Cloud*, one of the company's tour boats, with Benny, a veteran river pilot.

It was the middle of February. Seering and Kenny pulled up to The White Cloud, sitting in dry dock under two feet of snow. They took a ladder, climbed up onto the cold, slick deck and walked to the wheel.

"This is the wheel," Benny said, steam rising from his mouth with every word. He pulled his left hand out of his coat pocket. "This is '*Port.*' Turn the wheel to port." Seering turned the wheel to port. Benny pulled out his right hand.

"This is '*starboard.*' Turn the wheel to starboard." Seering turned the wheel to starboard.

They returned to the office.

"Yes, but how do I pass the test on rules of the road and buoy markings and all that?" inquired Seering. He was handed a document that contained every question ever asked on a U. S. Coast Guard 60 ton license examination along with the answers. Seering didn't ask how the answers had been procured.

"There is one more problem," Seering had said. "You have to have a minimum of 20/50 vision. I do not." Again, a document was produced with samples of every eye chart sold by every major medical and optometry supply house in the U.S. The first of thirty pages looked something like this

E

F P

T O Z|

L P E D

P E C F D

Memorize these came the instructions. On a cold Saturday morning in May, Seering drove to Milwaukee to sit for the exam. He found the address and walked in. The sign over the door had read:

OFFICER IN CHARGE OF MARINE INSPECTION

He went in and saw a gruff looking man in a uniform smoking the biggest cigar he had ever seen. Seering announced he was there to take his 60-ton pilot's license. The guy scrutinized him for a moment, then laughed.

"Son, this here is the Marines. The Coast Guard is down the hall! We *are* looking for a few good men though…" Seering nearly became One of the Few and the Proud.

The test turned out to be a piece of cake. Every question was familiar. So were the eye charts.

Finally a physical was required. The attending physician asked how Seering was feeling. Seering said he felt fine. The doctor wrote that down. Seering's heart rate was recorded and then he was asked how his hearing was. Seering said fine. The doctor wrote that down too.

Finally the doctor held up an orange and asked Seering what color it was. So ended the physical.

Seering actually turned into one of the best pilots on the river. After several "unauthorized" solo trips through the *Narrows* and into and out of notorious tight spots like *Cold Water Canyon*, producing a couple bent drive shafts and props, Seering found he was really developing a knack for it.

"The rest," concluded Wright and Mike the Bartender, "was history."

By the fourth and final drink of the night, the discussion had veered back to river guides and it was decided that Lower Dells tour guide Dan "The Golden Palomino" Dahlquist probably had had the most beautiful presentation on the river. After the last rock formation was pointed out, he would ask his captain to cut the boat's diesel engine and then in the silence, with only the lapping of the waters against the rocks and the boat, he would recite a poem he wrote quoting an old Indian chief:

*Every part of this soil is sacred
   in the estimation of my
people.
   Every hillside, every valley,
every plain and grove has been
hallowed by some sad or happy
   event in days long vanished.*

*Even the rocks, which seem
to be dumb and dead as they
swelter in the sun along the
silent shore, thrill with
  memories of stirring events
connected with the lives of
  my people.*

*And when the last red man
  shall have perished, and the
memory of my tribe shall become
a myth among the white men,*

these shores will swarm with
the invisible dead of my tribe.

At night when the streets of your
cities and villages are silent and
you think them deserted, they
will throng with the returning
hosts that once filled them and
still love this beautiful land.

The white man will never be alone.
  Let him be just and kindly with
  my people, for the dead are not
  powerless.

Dead did I say?

There is no death, only a changing
  of worlds.

Then Dahlquist would hit them all for a buck- fifty per guidebook.

****

The impending volleyball showdown at Bare Ass Beach between the Okids and the Winnebagos had become the talk of the town. The Okids felt that the main thing shouldn't be winning or loosing, it should be how they played the game.

They would play the game duplicitously.

First, it was decided that since the early scouting reports from Stand Rock indicated that most of Highridge's players were male, and since 80 percent of Team OKID were female, team OKID should have the skimpiest uniforms possible. Bikinis were acceptable. Less was better.

Next, Indian chants of "Pinko" would <u>not</u> be acceptable. To this end, Seering and Liz came up with the idea of coating all Okid team members in Okid yellow body paint.

Last but not least, Schneider was able to recruit a "ringer"- Pete Waite, his oldest friend, who was at that time a volleyball player at Ball State University. Waite would later go on to coach The University of Wisconsin woman's team to the NCAA finals. All of this of course, was top secret.

When the OKID pulled up to Bare Ass Beach on that fateful Sunday, Team Okid was confident of victory.

The first thing they found upon disembarking at Bare Ass was a regulation volleyball net and standards, which Waite immediately confirmed was one of the finest available. They didn't even want to know how the Winnebagos pulled that off. Evidently the Okid's puny little beach volleyball set wasn't going to be good enough for today's blood match.

Seering reassured everyone.

"Wait until we put on the Okid body paint."

Wright's washtub was placed in the sand next to the river's edge and gallons of yellow latex paint and bottle after bottle of dishwashing liquid (to ensure the paint would come off) was mixed until ready for application. A pleasant lemon scent filled the air.

The sight of the OKID women slathering up their bikini-clad bodies in yellow paint by the river disrupted the Winnebago's warm-ups. In fact, it was temporarily forgotten that there was a volleyball game to be played at all.

Soon the Winnebagos accused the OKIDs of stealing their war paint and Indian war cries were heard up and down the river.

The match started slowly, each side taking stock of the other. Like a good pool shark, Pete Waite did a good job early on of disguising his true abilities.

What he couldn't disguise was a genuine amazement in the lack of ability of his teammates. He simply could not stop laughing, and Schneider told him to shut up or he wouldn't be allowed to come back next week.

About half way through the match, Schneider started to itch. Looking around, he noticed his OKID teammates doing the same, looking generally uncomfortable. This grew more and more troublesome until a timeout had to be called. Only the Okids seemed to be affected. It was becoming unbearable. The Okids accused the Winnebagos of invoking some ancient curse. The Winnebagos accused the Okids of stalling.

Finally Highridge sniffed the air, and it occurred to everyone that the lemon in the dish soap was doing a number on the Okids' mucus membranes. A yellow geyser erupted from the river as everyone from Team *OKID* hit the water at once, while the Winnebagos watched and whooped with laughter.

The game ended up in a contested 2-point victory for the Okids, with the Winnebagos vowing revenge. They made a real ceremony out of vacating Bare Ass Beach en masse, matching anything the tourists would pay for up at Stand Rock, and promised that "the white man hasn't seen the last of us, etc..."

All this, of course, only after the beer had run out.

****

"Just listen to the wind blow...
let it   blow, let it blow-
WopShooAhh."
- Marshall Tucker

It was around 11:45 that evening that Wisconsin Dell's history was made.

Seering had just "punched out"- figuratively that is. As a practical matter, Seering was *always* working while on the River Inn premises, but around this time, after dining room closed, he would usually grab a drink and head in to the bar to make sure things were going ok. He would be there if needed for anything. Otherwise he was "off duty" 'till morning.

Schneider was up on his barstool singing to a near capacity crowd. The dining room had done well for a Sunday, and the bar receipts looked to be good as well. Wright and Joel had stopped by again to sit in the last set, and most of the Okids and regulars were floating in for a nightcap. Seering had just taken a seat at an open table and was joined by Tammy, then later by Kathy and Nemo.

Suddenly there was a commotion at the main lounge entrance and Seering looked up to see what appeared to be the entire cast of the Stand Rock Indian Ceremonial in full dress regalia heading down the stairs. They were carrying a huge Indian drum that had to be seven feet in diameter. Schneider noticed to his chagrin that even with the drum no one was have problems negotiating the steps.

Seering greeted Randy Highridge and was introduced to Randy's grandmother, Alberta Day. After extra tables were found for the Winnebagos, Schneider sang *Yellow Thunder* as a tribute to Mrs. Day. Then Seering lead the Okids in three cheers for their vanquished brothers. The first round from the bar was on the Okids.

There had always been an uneasy alliance between the Winnebagos and the rest of the town's residents, and bigotry sometimes had exposed its ugly, ignorant face. Tonight however, the River Inn played host to a reunion of brothers and sisters of different color, who shared a common regard for this place.

Alberta Day presented Seering with a yellow feather, proclaiming the Okids true friends of the Ho-Chunk ("Winnebago" in their tribal language).

Then the drums came out and they danced.

The Winnebagos taught the Okids the snake dance and the peace dance. Soon everyone was circling the bar, with the great drum being struck by committee in the center.

Closing time came, so the Winnebagos and the Okids and the drums and the dancing continued in the parking lot, spilling out onto River Road.

As he danced, Seering felt Tammy take his hand and heard her whisper in his ear.

He could still hear the Indian drums pounding in the distance as they drove away, the River Inn receding in the rear-view mirror of his ragtop MG, its nose pointed towards the rising sun of a brand new day.

6

**"Hot down, summer in the city- back
of my neck feelin' dirty and gritty"**
- *J. Sebastian*

The concept was born on a hot, muggy
Wednesday morning as Seering worked
behind the bar. July was nearly over and
August was predicted to be the warmest on
record. Outside, the heat and humidity fed
the growing cumulus clouds and they
climbed higher and higher over the river as
Seering watched them through the windows
between chores. There wasn't a breath of
wind, yet something was brewing.

Seering was filling in for Mike, who
was battling another bout of recurring car
problems and couldn't get in to work that
morning. The River Inn's air conditioner was
proving impotent in the swelter, and the
doors to the deck constantly opening and

closing didn't help matters any.   While sweating in the rising heat, Seering was feeling great- and shitty.

He and Tammy were really getting to know each other. The more he learned about her, the more he liked. She excited him. He smiled when he thought about the night of the Winnebagos visit to the River Inn and how Tammy had turned out to be more perfect than he had even imagined. He remembered swapping old photo albums with her the next morning- he looking at hers and she looking at his. Hers was a trip to Europe the previous summer. The photo that stood out most in Seering's mind was of Tammy in Paris, directing traffic under the *Arch de Triumph* with an umbrella. This was a woman he *had* to get to know better. He could see some real problems on the horizon, however.

First, he was Tammy's boss and he knew a manager should never get romantically involved with a staff member.

Second, she was a bit younger than he was. He was sure that there would be disapproving glances thrown his way but he didn't care. He was professional enough to handle the business side. Besides, it wasn't exactly Wall Street we were talking here, and she was a temporary employee. The age difference wasn't large enough to matter-he'd work his way through it. He had to. He really cared for this girl.

There was a larger problem, however. He was already dating two other girls, and one of them was the owner's daughter.

"Here we go again," he muttered out loud. Seering had always possessed an intriguing and somewhat unique approach to love and romance.

On the one hand, he enjoyed the company of a variety of women and yet on the other, he was a hopeless romantic who needed the emotional intimacy of one woman at a time. He had always been honest about this conundrum, this-- duplicity, yet his subsequent juggling always led to trouble. He just liked having fun.

Now he felt as if he may just have met his match in Tammy, and it scared him.

The bar was empty but there were several tables out on the deck with people looking for an early lunch. Seering had set up an outside grill and tables for lunchtime. This, combined with the bar sandwiches, kept the place going between the dining room's breakfast and dinner shifts.

Someone on the deck had just ordered another Banana Daiquiri. *What a horrible thing to do to a perfectly good drink*, Seering thought, as Joel Ireland walked in and sat down.

"*Loosen your lips, let out a yell- our kind of punk it raises hell…*"
                              - J. England

"Dan, I need the apartment for a while tonight." Said Joel. That was code for *I want to entertain a new young lady friend so please make yourself scarce for a couple hours.*

"No problem. I gotta work." Seering grinned. "How many tonight, *Bluebeard?*" the irony of his commentary escaping him.

Ireland just shrugged. Joel "Gold" Ireland was an honest-to- God true gentleman bachelor. Nobody ever heard a detail first hand, but where there was smoke there was almost certainly fire.

Joel was a handsome man with impeccable manners and taste. He was a trained landscape architect, but he continued to work part time as an entertainer up at the Showboat- the same job that had paid for his college. It had proven to be a source of an endless stream of women. Ireland was no scoundrel, but after a while it was impossible for Seering not to notice the women marching in and out of Joel's room in the apartment. They were always smiling.

They would give Seering a playful kiss on the cheek on the way in and ask if Joel was around.

Not even the help was immune. Seering, Ryker and Joel had employed a maid to come in once a week to vacuum and tidy up the kitchen and bedrooms. After a while it was becoming apparent that the maid's two and a half hours a week were being spent in Joel's room exclusively.

One day, after the maid had left, Seering's curiosity had gotten the best of him and he confronted Ireland.

"Again tonight? Jeez, Joel, I'm paying for some of this you know- how do you keep up? How do you keep them straight? WHAT DO YOU DO TO THESE WOMEN?!"

Ireland had shrugged and, after cutting Seering a check for his share of the maid's time, had quickly changed the subject. Seering could see it was a distasteful exercise for Ireland to discuss one's love life even obliquely with a buddy.

The rumors persisted, however. Seering knew it was juvenile, but a couple million years of evolution hadn't squelched his male curiosity.

Seering harbored a growing antipathy at Joel's ability to pull all this off while avoiding the snafus and hard feelings that Seering's multiple relationships inevitably produced. His thoughts finally turned back to more practical matters.

"By the way Joel, I've got a wedding party booked next Saturday and need a band. They're asking for swing and bluegrass music. Any ideas?"

"Sure. Wright can play bass on his washtub and I'll play mandolin. Have Schneider dust off his drum set so we can do some dance music, and there's a great new lead guitar player up at the Showboat who's been trolling for additional work. If I can find someone to fill in for us the last set at the Showboat, we could do it."

"Great," said Seering. "I'll talk to Wright and Schneids. Let me know if you can get the guitar player.

Seering walked to the kitchen to get a couple bananas. As he crossed to the produce locker, he could see his pastry cook, a wonderful elderly lady that had prepared the River Inn's breads and pastries for years, starting some banana bread. In front of her was a batch of old bananas to be used in her famous recipe.   "Those are the baddest bananas I ever saw Lucille," smiled Seering. "The badder the better," she smiled back. "Where are the fresh ones? I need some for the bar."

"Here you go partner," she said, swinging around with two choice yellow ones and pointing them at Seering as if drawing them out of a holster.

He took them back out to the bar. Ireland had poured himself a glass of iced tea from the cooler and had placed a couple dollars on the bar as he retook his seat. He reached for a bar nap to wipe his brow. The air was dead still. It looked to be turning into one lazy, hazy day. Seering sliced the bananas and mixed the daiquiris.

"You know," said Joel, apparently bored and with nothing else to do, "I never could get to like bananas."

"You should see the ones Lucille is using to make banana bread. I think they could kill. In fact, she drew 'em on me like out of a holster, Seering laughed.

"Bad?"

"Baddest bananas I've ever seen."

Ireland stretched back in his seat, imitating an old gunslinger. He was getting punchy, like Seering.

Neither spoke for several minutes. The air conditioner rattled along, trying to stir up the stagnant air.

"Your baaaar bananas look OK..."

More silence.

"Yeahupp," grinned Seering, picking up the slow cowboy drawl. "Ain't No Baaad Bar Bananas around here."

Seering placed a little paper umbrella in each drink and took them out to the deck. Another blast of clammy air invaded the lounge as Seering came back in. He went to the kitchen and came out with two more bananas.

"Thooose are bigggg," continued Joel in his low cowboy voice, the heat and the

132

humidity and the dead air now distilling a giddiness that was becoming contagious.

"Big Bananas."

"Big Barrr Bananas"

"Big BAD Barrr Bananas." Now they were giggling.

"BIG BAR ALL STAR BAAAAAAD BANANAS! They were laughing uncontrollably now, like two schoolboys on a hot playground. Just then Wright walked in.

"Anyone seen Kerri? Hey what's all the giggling about?"

"Dave, just the man we need to see," said Seering. "Want to join a band? I need some music for a wedding party next Saturday. Joel suggested you for washtub bass."

"That might be fun- what do we call ourselves?"

"Waaale…," Seering continued in his own cowboy voice, thar lookin' fer some bluegrass music. Bluegrass an' western swing- y'know -cowboy stuff.

"At a wedding?"

"Shore. That's whyyy we thought of yew on washtub. Schneids'll play drums, Joel can play mandolin or banjo."

"A bunch of Dells All Stars huh?" laughed Wright.

"You got it pardner" drawled Joel. "The Big Bar... All Star----- BAD BANANA BAND!"

Seering thought a moment.

"Hey, you know- that could work. We could offer specials on banana flavored drinks; we'll serve Lucile's banana bread-whatever."

"Do we know any bluegrass music?" asked Wright logically.

"A little country, some old folk music, some dixie stuff from the Showboat, maybe a little rock and roll thrown in- we'll make our own brand- like fusion or punk."

"Great. Like *country... punk you mean?*"

"Yeah, that's it," recited Seering. *The Big Bar All Star Bad Banana Band* plays *Country Punk* for your dining and dancing pleasure!"

Wright looked at Ireland. Then he looked at Seering.

He pulled a handkerchief out of his back pocket and wiped the back of his neck.

"What have you guys been drinking?"
****

Friday morning came and the swelter continued. The Big Bar All-Star Bad Banana Band gathered at the River Inn's apartment to practice. They needed to put a set list together. Seering served his famous Harvey Wall bangers to keep the band hydrated. It was that kind of day.

The music came together quickly and by noon they decided to take their instruments down to the pontoon boat and continue ironing out the rough spots on the river. As the Bad Bananas practiced, Seering drove the OKID up-river past Black Hawk Island and entered the narrows.

"*Salty Dog*" ricocheted off the walls of the Elbow.

Later, *Cold Water Canyon* came into view and Seering decided to cool off and give the tourists in the tight little docking area some music. *Cold Water Canyon* was one of several "Brigutary Glens" that got its name from the drop in temperature (as much as ten degrees) experienced when one entered the little gorge by water. They entered the same skinny little dead-end that Seering had terrorized as a tour boat captain years ago and turned around while serenading the blank-faced visitors.

The visit lasted longer than anticipated, the boys enjoying the respite from the heat and the Canyon's visitors enjoying the music.

Then it was on to the Great Bay and *Stand Rock* before heading back down-river through the Old River Bed.

As the Okid reentered the main channel at Black Hawk Island, a sheriff's boat and two rigid hulled inflatables could be seen slowly circling between the "Jaws" of *High Rock* and *Romance Cliff*, and the River Inn.

Schneider watched and wondered what could be happening until they got a little farther down-river and he saw something else that completely stole his attention, something he hoped Wright hadn't noticed. An obviously enraptured couple was frolicking in the water off the east end of Bare Ass Beach. One of them was Kerri Reasonor.

****

"If anyone wants to know where my heart is, tell everyone
that it's wrapped around yours…"
    - G. Nash

This weekend's special:
<u>Magnum</u>
<u>Banana Daiquiri</u>
$3.50
If you don't like it,
throw it at the entertainer!

Schneider picked the stack of notices off the bar, read them and winced.

"They're going on every table in the lounge and the restaurant as soon as Liz is through, said Mike. "Seering's idea."

Swell. Nice job, Seering- Thanks. That's all I need.

Tomorrow night was the wedding party, but Seering evidently couldn't wait to get started on his *Bad Banana* promotion.

It was early, so Schneider ordered dinner and walked out to the deck in the twilight. It had cooled down considerably from that afternoon- maybe a storm coming.

There was a thin layer of steam fog rising from the tepid river water.

That was funny, thought Schneider. *What was the Clipper doing anchored off High Rock?* Being the largest of the tour boats, The *Clipper Winnebago* was usually used as a water taxi to the Indian Ceremonial on Friday nights. *It should be docked up at Stand Rock by now. What was it doing sitting out there?*

There was just enough light to indicate the big tour boat was now getting closer. As it did, Schneider could begin to make out a pilot in the wheelhouse but very few others on board. Schneider looked again and squinted. The Clipper wasn't anchored - it was dragging something while drifting down river. He watched it until it got just off the River Inn, where it lit up its engines and motored back up off High rock and started to drift again.

He came back into the lounge wondering what was going on. As he did so, Liz- *God, she looked good tonight*- started a song that diverted his train of thought entirely.

You brought out the sun in me,
You made me feel so fine.
You brought out the fun in me,
I wanted you for mine...

Schneider thought for a moment. He had gotten a couple more notes from his "secret admirer" in the past week. *Maybe*-no, impossible. No chance. Someone was just playing games with him, since it was obvious to everyone by now how he felt about her. What they couldn't know however, was how deep it went.

The last evening he had off, Schneider had gone to the cabin at Sunset Lodge Liz had rented for the summer. They had been learning a couple new songs. Afterwards they had talked for a while until it became obvious it was time for him to go. Leaving that cabin was the hardest thing he had done in a long while. If he could only have stopped the clock- content to simply talk and make music with this girl, he'd have gladly done so- for the rest of his life. He wanted to tell her his whole life's story. He wanted to hear hers.

This was not an infatuation or a simple case of lust. Schneider treasured every moment he spent with her. Why couldn't she feel the same?

He thought about how he had run across Joe Redmund, who was also living at Sunset Lodge, on his way out. Redmund had been sitting at a campfire in the Lodge's outdoor fire pit, after having built the most enormous Martini Schneider had ever seen. He was sipping it "neat" in a huge martini glass with a single olive and was wearing a tee shirt made to look like a tuxedo. He stared into the fire while drinking his *James Bond* dry martini in his tuxedo tee shirt.

"All dressed up with nowhere to go, Joe?" Schneider had asked as he passed. Redmund had merely nodded and stared into the fire with those lonely eyes of his.

I know the feeling Schneider had thought to himself before turning to go.

Schneider sat down at the bar and asked Mike for a pen. He grabbed a bar nap and scribbled out the first lines of a song he would write for Liz. He still hadn't lost hope.

As you sang the song about
how he let the sun out in you
I thought, with her
what an easy thing to do

And I hope that you're not
frightened by this song
But the music that you play
makes me want to sing along.
And I hope that you remain a song.

****

Once again Liz and Schneider did their thirty minutes together, and then once again Schneider was alone. It was dark outside now, but from his vantage point he could still see the *Clipper*, her powerful bow lantern now cutting through the thin fog and into the black water. It glowed like a specter, coming and going.

Bernie Colsen and Bob Bleighman walked in from the dining room just as the cocktail waitress was placing the *"Throw it at the Entertainer"* placards on the tables. The mayor read one, smiled, paused to give

Schneider *the look,* then shook his head and followed Bleighman to the bar. Wright walked in from the dining room at the same moment and took his usual seat near the waitress station. He didn't look happy.

In fact, the whole lounge seemed somewhat subdued tonight. Every now and then, someone would turn and look out towards the *Clipper* and her searchlight, cutting through the fog. Suddenly, Schneider put the pieces from that afternoon together and shuddered. He took a break and walked to the bar.

"You've been through this before, haven't you?" he asked Dave Wright, motioning out to the *Clipper.*

"Yeah. I was in having dinner just now but couldn't eat. Dan finally pulled the shades after word got around."

"Do you know what happened?"

"Some kid jumped off High Rock this afternoon. His buddies never saw him come up."

"Why the *Clipper?*"

"It's the widest boat on the river. Lots of room for gear and all. They can drag more lines... I guess." Wright ordered a double and Schneider joined him.

Schneider turned to walk over to Colsen but saw he was talking grimly, officially, to a uniform who had joined him and decided against it. He turned back to Wright.

"How long do they stay out? The *Clipper* I mean."

"Couple days. If they don't find anything by then--

"Jesus."

"Yeah." Wright took a long sip and paused until Schneider had sat down next to him.

"Kerri and I are done."

Shit, that didn't take long, thought Schneider.

He didn't know what to say, so he didn't say anything.

That didn't happen very often.

7

The *Clipper* was gone when Schneider woke the next morning. Saturday. He walked over to look out the windows of his room immediately after waking. He knew that what he had seen the previous night would haunt him for a long time, but now there were other things to tend to.

The Bad Bananas were playing that evening, and Joel had scheduled a rehearsal for noon in the banquet room, which was really just an extension of the dining room with a heavy partition that could be opened or closed. Seering knew the bride well (another former girlfriend) and had asked her if it was OK to open the partition around 9:30 and offer the music to the rest of the Inn's patrons. The bride came from a prominent local family and knew everyone in town anyway, so she had agreed.

The Big Bar All Star Bad Banana Band's debut promised to be a wild and crazy good time. After the events of last night, everyone would be ready to let their hair down a bit.

Schneider had dishwashing duty that morning, and he walked down to the kitchen. The storm that seemed imminent the night before had failed to materialize and now this morning seemed like a repeat of yesterday. Hot, muggy, perhaps something starting to brew up again.

The dining room was not very busy, but the kitchen was abuzz with excitement. Two rumors were floating around.

The first was that the River Inn was being sold. Representatives from some syndicate in Cleveland were in town to look the place over.

The second was that famous rock stars were staying at the River Inn. The Dave Miller Band, a group enjoying enormous current success, was playing Madison the next day. The band had gotten its start playing the Minneapolis- Milwaukee- Chicago club circuit before hitting it big. In those days the band had played a regular gig at a big dance club west of town and knew the area well. The scuttlebutt was that the boys were enjoying a couple days off before the Madison concert, and they were staying at the River Inn.

How the rumor got started was anyone's guess, but in the course of putting three loads of dishes through the big Hobart Schneider had heard the following:

a) Someone matching the description of Dave Miller himself was in the bar last night (if he was, Schneider hadn't noticed).

b) The band's lead singer had been seen poolside, hustling every skirt in sight and/or

c) The entire band had torn up room 238 the previous night.

Schneider was just finishing his shift when one of the young breakfast waitresses came in, gushing that she had heard the band was going to be at the wedding reception tonight- friends of the groom or some such thing. Schneider had to admit it was an exciting prospect. He wiped down the dishwasher and went out to the lounge for a Coke before his rehearsal began.

Allison and Redmund were at the bar grabbing a quick sandwich between trips.

"Frank, Joe"

"How's it going Dave?"

"Same oh same oh-What's the word on the river? Did the Clipper find what it was looking for last night?"

"No. They gave up just after dawn. We'll just have to wait"-- Allison didn't finish the sentence.

"They'll be keeping an eye peeled around the dam for a couple days though" added Redmund.

"Was the kid local?"

"No, up from Evanston with some friends evidently."

"Don't imagine there'll be anyone jumping off High Rock for a while," commented Schneider.

"Are you kidding?" said Redmund. "We saw two go off this morning's trip. Everyone wants to be a hero. Impress the ladies."

"Old fools aren't always the biggest fools." Added Allison, shaking his head.

****

"I'm alright- don't nobody worry 'bout me..."
-K. Loggins

The heat and humidity again was building. On his way out of the lounge, Schneider overheard Seering talking on the bar's phone, sounding very defensive. Things like *"but-"* and *"I know, but-"*- that sort of thing. At one point, Seering took the phone from his ear and Schneider could hear what sounded like a female chipmunk on the other end of the line. Probably Lynn Shank.

Lynn was the third peg in Seering's current triad. *Here we go again*, thought Schneider, well aware of his good friend's romantic foibles.

The *Night of the Winnebagos* and Seering's growing relationship with Tammy was finally catching up with him. Schneider recalled a few weeks before, and the *OKID Champagne Golf Classic*, another Seering idea that had gotten him in trouble. It had consisted of the OKID men hacking away while golf cart- mounted boom boxes blared the theme to *Caddyshack,* and the OKID women, dressed in cheerleader outfits, drove the carts around serving champagne to the competitors.

Lynn, who had taken exception to Seering's choice of cheerleaders, had later punched him out in the clubhouse Men's Room. Who could blame her? How could a man so blatantly sexist, so profoundly hedonistic as Seering *not* be in constant trouble with women?

Schneider knew it had something to do with Seering's own internal combustion of megalomania and selflessness- his own personal alchemy of recklessness and insight. He wasn't cavalier, nor was he insensitive. He was simply- Seering. He always gave something unique, something special, just as he did now, sharing his singular recipe for enjoying life with the OKIDs.

Seering wasn't tall or especially good-looking, but having fun was very sexy, and Dan was seldom alone in his constant quest to redefine how to enjoy life. He made up his own rules. And they worked. Every now and then however, they produced some fireworks as well.

Sometimes Seering had gotten into trouble even when he was innocent. Schneider remembered the weekend that his sister Debi's old friend Katy Dent came for a weekend visit. Katy and Dan had dated throughout their teens but hadn't seen each other for years. Katy was in an unhappy marriage in New York and during a cruise up river told Dan about it. She asked if they could "get together" the following weekend and Dan had declined, citing her marital status.

The following day, Seering's father showed up at the River Inn and told Dan that he had received a call from a Paul Shaver in New York. Mr. Shaver informed the elder Seering that his son was sleeping with his wife and that he had a gun and was coming after him. Then he had hung up.

Being a Judge, Seering's father was not a stranger to threats and always took them seriously. He correctly assumed that his son wouldn't sleep with another man's wife, but nevertheless was concerned.

That day Dan had called Katy and asked her how her husband could have thought such a thing. Katy told him that her husband was very jealous and, in the past, had hired private investigators to follow her. She had said it was very possible there would be trouble. Nothing ever happened, but the

River Inn apartment had had some extremely light sleepers for a while. Schneider thought about this and watched as Seering quietly hung up the phone from yet another snafu and looked his way.

"That was Debbie," Seering said. "She knows about Tammy. And she's coming over."

"Wonderful." responded Schneider.

"That's not the worst part. Lynn called earlier. She's in the wedding so she'll be here too."

Schneider and his old friend collectively shook their heads.

Here we go again.

****

***"The summer wind
came rolling in..."***
-J. Mercer

Schneider stood on his roof -top deck, taking one last look behind him at the setting sun and wondered if he should wear a suit. He had planned to for the wedding reception tonight, but that was before Seering had declared Frozen Drink Wars. He decided to chance it. He would play an early set with Liz, then one alone, followed by the Bad Bananas in the dining room/banquet hall for the reception.

He thought about tonight. Would the Dave Miller Band really show up? How about the prospective buyers from Cleveland? Was that on the level? And how was Seering going to handle Tammy, Lynn, and Debbie Klinke (not to mention Debbie's father) all in the same place at the same time?

It had started to cool off again- just like last night- only more so, and Schneider could see the vinyl tablecloths and deck umbrellas on the deck below starting to flap in the quickening breeze. He shivered. Something was definitely starting to brew again- perhaps this time to boil over into one hell of a storm.

****

The rest of the Bad Bananas' All Stars were in the lounge when Schneider came downstairs that evening. Something   very interesting happened after his set with Liz-she gave him a quick peck on the cheek before leaving the stage.

Was it just a "stage kiss" or a hint?

It had become obvious how Schneider felt about her, but she still hadn't exhibited any interest- or attachments. For all Schneider knew, she could be the most beautiful *lesbian* alive, but she hadn't hinted at *that* either.   Nevertheless,   at   that moment Schneider was so spellbound he didn't notice the young bridesmaid walking by the stage in her formal. Seconds later, something happened that would cause Schneider to temporarily forget all about Liz.

An old high school buddy had come up to surprise him that night and was hiding behind the bar. He had seen the *"Throw it at the Entertainer"* hand bills and chose that precise moment to surprise his good friend.

Schneider looked up in time to see someone leaping out from behind the bar and launching an entire Daiquiri in his direction. It turned into a full frontal assault on the bridesmaid.

****

Schneider stared in disbelief. So did the bridesmaid.

Schneider's friend apologized and Seering insisted on the River Inn paying for the dry cleaning bill, but the poor girl was still understandably irked. Seering had a couple waitresses take her off and help clean her up. Soon the incident was forgotten. Schneider, however, continued to keep his eyes peeled for flying Daiquiris.

There had been no sign of any rock stars yet. No flashbulbs going off, no screaming fans, no obnoxious behavior. Seering had told Schneider that if they were staying at the River Inn, they were doing so under false names and identification because he knew nothing about it. And he hadn't heard of any problems in room 238 either. He thought the whole thing highly unlikely.

Nevertheless it appeared the rumor had spread uptown as well, for the River Inn started to host a continuous flow of kids coming in and out. This, in addition to the wedding reception provided for a highly charged full house that evening. If there were people on the premises acting as agents for those Cleveland buyers, this would be a good night for them to look around.

****

The Bad Bananas were in full swing by the time Seering got his first inkling of trouble. Tammy had the night off but she had come in to see him and catch a little of the *Bad Bananas*. She had heard about Reasonor's escapade off Bare Ass Beach and figured Wright might need some cheering up as well.

As she was exiting the ladies' room, Debbie Klinke was walking by on her way in.

"You're Tammy, aren't you? I'm Debbie Klinke."

"Nice to meet you, Debbie."

"You're a bit young, aren't you?"

"I beg your pardon?"

"For Dan."

"Seering? We're just having a good time. He's a nice guy."

"Yes, but he's my guy."

"No, he's my guy." They turned to see Lynn Shank. She had been heading to the ladies' room and joined the conversation. Lynn continued "and what are you going to do about it?" She moved in a bit so she could be heard.

"Let me give you a suggestion..." whispered Tammy.

The discussion continued.

****

The swelter finally broke and produced a thunderstorm that rattled the River Inn to its foundation.

At the bar, Frank Allison smiled. "They trapped him into damaging revealments, eh?" he asked Nemo, once again invoking Twain. Nemo laughed and looked back towards the Rest Rooms. The Ladies were still discussing their differences, but now giggles were starting to replace threats. Nemo would continue to monitor the situation.

Out front, the Bad Bananas were jamming away through their last set. The bride and groom had both let their hair down- literally- and were now clogging away in bare feet out on the dance floor with the rest of their guests. Only in *The Dells*.

The Dave Miller Band had failed to materialize, but the prospective buyers from Cleveland had, and they seemed a bit too well dressed. Silk suits and pinky rings, Seering had told Nemo. This didn't exactly alleviate anyone's anxieties about the Fire Inspector's earlier warnings. The evening wore on.

The Bad Bananas finally finished their last number and everyone sat down to relax as the crowd filtered out. Later they would begin the cleanup so that Sunday Brunch could commence on time in another seven hours. Schneider had custodian duty tonight as well.

As Seering started to help clear the dining room tables, Tammy, Lynn and Debbie all appeared at the swinging doors from the Kitchen. Each carried a piece of wedding cake. They split up and started to approach Seering from different angles.

Schneider could see what was happening and sat down on his drum stool to watch. He motioned over the rest of the band. "This should be good…" he predicted.

At this moment, Seering recognized what was happening and dove for cover under a table. A millisecond later, the table was creamed by an incoming barrage of cake and icing.

Schneider could see that Seering was going to get away unscathed, which he could not allow to happen. He sprinted to the kitchen and picked up the last piece of wedding cake, then proceeded to dive out the kitchen doors and launch just as Seering was climbing out of his "foxhole". The cake hit him square in the face.

"SCHNEIDER, YOU IDIOT!!" roared Seering.

"Jeez, lighten up Seering, it's just a piece of cake in the face."

"Just a piece of cake?" You moron! You just destroyed the bride's traditional 'top of the cake!' Her whole family has the river deck reserved here tomorrow morning at eleven - for coffee and wedding cake!

****

Once again Schneider was transformed from entertainer to cleanup crew. Once again, Schneider felt like the only living cell in a dead body as he headed down the "tunnel" towards the rest rooms. The building's downstairs was empty, and thunder continued to reverberate through its innards.

Schneider's mind was filled with foreboding. He thought about Seering's orders to replace the top of the wedding cake before 11:00 the next morning. He wondered if Tammy, Debbie and Lynn were regrouping for another attack. If so, how so?

He also thought about those greasy guys from Cleveland. Surely Ken Klinke would refuse to hand over the River Inn to that bunch of slimeballs. Maybe *they* were the ones responsible for those suspicious canisters.

A flash of brilliant light swept through the tunnel accompanied by a *"snap"* and a deafening crack of thunder that shook the old structure. One more graveyard janitorial shift was nearly over. Just the bathrooms and Schneider would be finished.

Good, thought Schneider. *This storm is giving me the heebie-jeebies.* It was now 3:30am. He froze as he once again thought he heard something.

Nothing.

He rolled the cart to the end of the hall, pushed the door to the Men's Room open and was immediately confronted by a man directly in front of him.

****

The man was sitting on the john, the door to the stall wide open.

"*Jesus Christ!*" exclaimed Schneider, ready to slam the door shut and run for his life. It was obvious, however,

that the poor bastard was in the bathroom for a reason, drunk as a skunk.

"Bar time was two hours ago. How long have you been sitting here?" Schneider asked the man, who looked to be homeless.

"Thought I might stick around a bit- do it all the time. What's say me and you check out your kitchen," the man said, trying to stand up and failing. Schneider suggested to him that he pull up his trousers and join him in the hallway. He figured he'd escort the poor old drunk out through the dining room and the main exit, but the guy took a left into the kitchen and headed for the walk-in freezer. He was starting to resist Schneider's hand on his arm and Schneider was getting ready to phone the police when he got an idea.

"How 'bout we grab a sandwich out at the bar?" Schneider suggested.

"Lead the way friend."

Schneider took the man out to the lounge and gave him one of the bar sandwiches kept in the cooler.

The man wanted to sit and enjoy his sandwich with a beer but Schneider managed to walk him up and out of the lounge and into the parking lot. The storm was retreating now, and the rain had been reduced to drizzle. The last Schneider saw of him, the old fart was heading up River Road towards Broadway munching on his sandwich.

When Schneider finally finished the bathrooms, he heard intonations similar to fingernails scratching a blackboard coming from the kitchen, and checking his watch, figured that Ryker was starting Sunday Brunch preparations while singing along to his beloved 8-track tapes of *Jules Blattner and the Warren Groovy All-star Band.*

****

7:50 AM-Schneider wakes after less than 4 hours of sleep. He has to get to the local grocery store, find a cake similar to the one he destroyed, and get it back in time to do whatever modifications were necessary to pass it off as the real thing before the bride's family arrived. He would start at Ken Klinke's IGA. He is prepared, however, to expand the search if necessary.

8:58 AM- The grocery store opens and Schneider is the first through the doors. He heads immediately to the bakery section and finds what looks to be the same kind of white cake and icing. It is square, but could be cut round and trimmed with extra icing. After picking out a couple different brands of vanilla icing, Schneider takes it all back to the River Inn.

Brunch is being served and the dining room is half full by the time Schneider and the cake arrive back at the kitchen. He cuts the cake round, mixed up both icings, chooses one and finishes off the cake. Just then Seering walks in.

"What do you think?" asks Schneider.

"Schneids, it was nice of you to go through the trouble, but we're still screwed. The original had writing on it."

"Shit. What did it say and what color was the icing?"

"I don't have the foggiest. It came from Klinke's though."

9:55AM- back up to Klinke's Super Market. One hour to go. The baker has the day off but someone behind the counter remembers how the cake had been trimmed. Back to the River Inn with the proper colored icing for trimming.

10:30AM- they apply the trim.

10:47AM- It now occurs to Seering and Schneider that the original wedding cake probably had been photographed and observed by nearly everyone at the reception. The last thing they needed after all this was somebody saying, *"hey that's not your cake."*

To be on the safe side, Seering decides to cut the cake and serve it in pieces. As Seering starts cutting the cake, he spins around and it appears he might turn the knife on Schneider.

"Schneider you putz, didn't you check the date on this cake? It's stale."

"I guess I didn't notice. I was in such a hurry and all…"

11:01AM- the bride's family starts to arrive and is seated out on the deck.

"Schneidy, go upstairs and ask the maid for the spray bottle. The one she mists the plants with," says Ryker. Schneider is bewildered.

"Go ahead."

Schneider does as he is told.

11:05AM- Schneider flies back down the steps into the kitchen and hands the spray bottle to Ryker. Ryker opens the top and sniffs it.

"Good," he says, emptying and refilling the spray bottle with fresh tap water. He sprays every piece of cake and puts them in the microwave for 10 seconds. He pulls out the tray of cake pieces and places them on a silver platter. They look and smell like they have just come out of a bakery.

Schneider falls to Ryker's feet as the cake is wheeled out, along with silver coffee service, to the assembled guests.

11:10AM- Applause is heard from the deck.

In the kitchen, everyone is on the floor.

8

"Oh Yeah........."
-The Kinks

The daydream was always the same, and it played through Schneider's mind again as he delayed getting out of bed.

State Street. Madison, Wisconsin; 1968.

There was a live rock band hammering out the Kinks' *You Really Got Me* at a Eugene McCarthy campaign rally just outside the University campus. Schneider was coming down the steps of Ziegler's Music Shop after trying the patience of his guitar teacher for another half-hour lesson. He carried his pride and joy- a replica Les Paul electric guitar his father had gotten him from Sears and Roebuck. He was ten years old.

Rather than wait upstairs for his father to pick him up like he usually did, Schneider followed the rock and roll music downstairs and next door to the rally. He sat and was mesmerized by the long hair and the microphones and the guitar cords and the cymbals. He'd never seen a live rock & roll band before.

Utter joy.

Goosebumps.Freedom.Consciousness.

Within six months his father would cut off the guitar lessons because Schneider wouldn't "practice the notes" and still couldn't read a bit of music. His son just wanted to play along to his sister's records.

But two years after *that* his father would buy him an Epiphone 12 string acoustic guitar and refuse to let him quit the school band when he wanted to. His father evidently knew something. He had *heard* something. Eventually that same guitar would pay for a college education.

Schneider reflected on this often, thankful for his father's wisdom and his mother's talent. And he would always remember that band on State Street playing *You Really Got Me.*

****

Schneider finally got out of bed and went to the windows to check on the river and the morning's weather. Both were still there.

August had arrived. The season was swinging into high gear, heading towards the climactic Labor Day weekend celebration. Schneider had heard many tales about the unofficial close to the Dells' tourist season and the eerie effect it had on the locals.

August, it was said, was just one big rehearsal for Labor Day weekend. Schneider showered and went downstairs. He was meeting Liz in the lounge to go over a new song. They were going to record a demo of it together.

He had decided that today he would go for it. After the rehearsal he would ask Liz if she would like to go out to Bare Ass Beach after work tonight- just the two of them. He *had* to know if she was the one writing the *secret admirer* notes.

As he walked into the lounge the phone rang and Mike picked it up. He called to Schneider.

"It's for you. They transferred it from upstairs."

"Thanks, Mike." Schneider picked up the phone. The call was from Scott Nabholz. Scott and Schneider had been in several working rock bands together throughout high school, and Scott had been the keyboard player for the infamous Holiday Party blowout at the River Inn last winter. He was now playing in a well-known show band that was booked up the river a bit at Chula Vista, the Dells' most upscale resort and nightclub.

Scott explained that one of the resort's long-time customers was celebrating his 65th birthday and the management needed someone to provide some music for a surprise dinner party. Scott was tied up so he had suggested Schneider. It would pay four times what Schneider usually made for an evening at the River Inn. And it was just for an hour and a half over dinner.

"What about a P.A.?" Schneider asked.

"You can use the band's. All you gotta bring is your guitar," answered Scott.

"You're on. When should I be there?"

"Five O'clock."

"What kind of stuff are they gonna want to hear?"

"O.F.S.- right up your ally." O.F.S stood for *Old Fart Shit.*

"Thanks Scott. Tell them I'll be there." *Man- scale times four and I can still be back in time for work here.* Seering walked in and went behind the bar to get something. Mike handed both of them an envelope.

"I wanted to invite you to a little party I'm throwing out at the farm, he said. "We're going to take some pictures."

Apart from his duties tending bar at the River Inn, Mike was an avid photographer, and occasionally got paid for doing commercial work. Back during his river boat days he had captured some breathtaking images of the river, one even ending up on a national travel log.

If truth be told, Mike could do some truly stunning work, but he didn't have the 'fire in the belly' to hustle his camera full time.

He grinned as Schneider and Seering opened the envelopes and took out the invitations. "My car died so I'm going to blow it up. We're gonna take pictures."

"Whatdaya mean?"

"I mean that car *done me wrong*. One of my roommates is an ex- Navy SEAL.

Worked demolition in Vietnam. He likes to blow things up. I like to take pictures. Logical, no?"

Seering looked at Schneider, then at Mike. "Mike, didn't you tell me you're still making payments on that car?"

"Yeah, well the payment book will be in the glove compartment. We're gonna have six F1's set up with motor drives, a couple of Hasselblads, a High 8 and even a 16 millimeter movie camera. I plan on winning the next *Dells Film Festival* with this. We'll have everything sync'd through a Mac using electronic cable releases and filtered through a ..."

Seering and Schneider looked at each other, then at Mike who was grinning ear to ear.

"We thought we might as well make a party out of it," he continued. Mike sounded very sincere.

"I've already applied for the permits. We're planning on ten half-barrels of beer and sixty pounds of dynamite."

****

While Seering and Schneider were contemplating what kind of a party ten half barrels of beer and 60 pounds of dynamite could produce, Liz walked in. She wore a white sundress that almost knocked the boys off their barstools.

"Shall we get started Schneidy?"

"Absolutely" was all Schneider could manage. They rehearsed their song, arranging the vocals and suggesting small changes here and there. They worked well together and enjoyed each other's company. Schneider felt there was no better time.

"Liz, I thought it might be nice to take a ride out to the Beach tonight. You know, take the guitars, maybe a bottle of wine- I hear there's supposed to be a big meteor shower tonight. We could watch the stars and write some music. What do you think?" He held his breath.

"Sure. What time do you want to go?"

That was too easy.

"After bar time, I guess. I'll ask Ken Klinke if we can borrow the Chris-craft. How's that sound?"

"Sounds great. See you tonight."

Liz left, leaving Schneider glued to his chair, mouth hanging open, absolutely numb.

****

That <u>was</u> too easy. Maybe she didn't know what she was doing, thought Schneider. *Maybe she didn't realize she was saying yes to a <u>date</u>. Maybe she thought she was merely going stargazing with a friend. Maybe she thought it was just a nice way to practice the music.*

Or maybe she was waiting for the offer all along. There still had been no hint of an attraction though.

"That's it," Schneider said out loud. "She didn't make a big deal out of it because she doesn't *think* it's a big deal."

"Schneider, you're muttering again- what's going on?" It was Seering.

"I just asked Liz out to Bare Ass tonight after work and she said yes."

"You're kidding."

"Nope. By the way, what's happening with Debbie and Lynn?" Schneider knew Seering liked both girls very much, but he also knew Tammy had truly stolen his heart. Something had to give.

"Neither one are speaking to me."

"Looks like your problems are solved," said Schneider, although he was not insensitive enough not to realize it was messier than that.

"Well I feel like shit, but what are you gonna do?"

"I don't know, but whatever it is, you'll probably do it again."

They both shrugged. "By the way, whatever happened with those buyers from Cleve--"

An explosion outside interrupted Schneider's question. Seering ran to the deck with Schneider close on his heels. The propane grill had caught fire and was shooting flames up into the deck above, threatening to set the building ablaze. Seering, Schneider, and the lunch cook grabbed the grill by the legs and together tipped it over the rail and into the river. A huge cloud of steam enveloped the deck and Seering quickly splashed some water on the overhead to ensure there were no embers to catch fire later. Customers who had fled to the other corner of the deck now came back and sat down, nervously discussing what had just occurred.

"Holy shit" said the cook.

"Shit is right," said Seering. "That was a twelve-hundred dollar stainless steal grill. King's gonna go nuts."

"Maybe our owners would have rather you let it burn," mused Schneider, immediately realizing what he had said. Seering shot him a nasty glance but said nothing.

"I may be able to find it," said the cook.

"Jay," said Seering "its sixty feet deep right off here, with God knows what kind of currents."

"I'm a scuba diver. I do this all the time."

"Really? Let me think about it. I appreciate the offer."

"Sure. What do we do now?"

"Better fire up the kitchen's broiler and fryer- not literally this time, OK?"

"Sure thing boss," laughed the kid as he headed inside.

****

"Just a little lovin' will go a long way..."
-   *E. Arnold*

Schneider walk into the Chula Vista Resort around 4:45. The lounge was huge by River Inn standards and was flanked by two large bars. The guest of honor had just been "surprised" and everyone was sitting down to eat. *Every* single head in the place had gray hair on it. Schneider estimated the crowd at 75 to 80 people. He placed his tip jar on the front of the stage, tuned up his guitar and plugged it into the PA system.

Schneider loved to indulge in the dangerous game of trying to figure out his audience's musical taste before singing a note. Tonight he would be successful beyond anything before or since. He started off with the old Jim Reeves hit *I Really Don't Want to Know*. He hit a home run. Every gray head was turning to another gray head and nodding approval. Some sang along. When he followed up with *Just a little lovin'* the dance floor immediately filled up.

What was the secret of his success with the over-60 crowd? Schneider truly enjoyed being around these older folks and he sincerely enjoyed their music. It took him back to his childhood when he would lay in bed and listen to his family's records at bedtime. His mother collected show tunes, jazz and standards- Judy Garland, Sarah Vaughn, Nancy Wilson, Ella. His father- just the opposite. Eddy Arnold, Jim Reeves, Hank Williams, Marty Robbins. Meanwhile his sister listened to the Beatles, Gene Pitney, Leslie Gore, The Rascals. Schneider loved it all.

Someone came up and dropped a buck in his tip jar while requesting another oldie, and by his fifth number folks were actually lining up along the side of the dance floor to request a song and put money in his jar. Schneider had never seen that before. He could absolutely *do no wrong*. He saw fives, tens, twenty's going in his jar. He played every *Old Fart* tune he knew. The hour and a half came to a close and the crowd *refused* to let Schneider leave. Some guy came forward and offered to put a *fifty* in the jar for another half-hour of music.

It was the most rewarding- and lucrative 2 hours of his musical life. Schneider was fortified by his success at

Chula Vista as he hurried back to the River Inn. He had an even bigger challenge awaiting him there- Liz.

****

Would that I were a butterfly
And you a sensuous flower,
With a heart of golden honey,
In an alabaster bower.
Just you and I, beneath a sky,
Of dancing stars and arrowed beams;
A winged sigh, a blossom nigh,
In the chapel of pagan dreams.

I'd creep amidst your scented tips,
In the glow of a moon canoe,
And madly sip from nectared lips,
The fatal brew of rose-red hue.
I'd slip within a petaled breast,
To breathe my last in bosom sweet;
Immortal lust, fore'er at rest,

With death and you, my cross
  and wreathe.
My soul would rise to skies above,
Our wings would blend
  with the stars...

-Capt. Don Saunders, 1946
Wisconsin Dells, WI
"When the Moon is a Silver Canoe."

"…and that old moon can still be
found ridin' in the desert sky…"
- Marshal Tucker Band

The old mahogany Chris Craft rumbled to life as Schneider turned the key. It was a warm, clear night. Not a cloud in the sky. The forecasted meteor shower promised to be spectacular if it stayed like this.

Schneider untied the lines while Liz put the guitars in the boat. Then came the cooler filled with wine and cheese and crackers. After Liz climbed in, everything in the world that Schneider needed to be happy was in that old runabout.

As the lights of the River Inn receded in the distance, the sky above turned from black to a deep blue and then white, with millions of stars coalescing into bands across the summer sky. Schneider felt the warm air blowing over his cheeks and arms and glanced over to the extraordinary girl beside him. He closed his eyes and opened them again. He wasn't dreaming.

The beach started to loom just ahead and Schneider cut the engine to idle, then shut it down. The boat slid up onto the sand and tilted over slightly to one side. The engine's low rumble was immediately replaced by utter silence. Schneider was pleased to see they were the only ones on the beach. By the time they had unloaded the guitars and placed the cooler near a suitable site for a fire, crickets and cicadas had joined the silence.

They built a small fire. Schneider opened the wine, then took out his guitar. Liz, sitting down next to him in the sand, brushed up against him. They played a couple songs together, then laid back to watch the stars. Liz leaned over and touched Schneider's shoulder.

"Can I ask you a question?"

"Sure," said Schneider, suddenly starting to sweat. Liz rose and turned, her breasts levitating near Schneider's chin as she looked down at him.

"How *did* Bare Ass Beach get its name?"

Just then a white light appeared on the river, followed seconds later by a green and red light, directly below it. Now they could hear an outboard motor: a boat coming straight towards them.

Schneider's heart sank. Now there were two boats- no three- heading for them. They could hear screaming and laughing. The armada landed on the beach and boatloads full of bar-time partiers disembarked.

The invasion had originated from Nigs, a stick-to-the-floor meat market/dance bar up on Broadway. Out of the boats jumped Clare the Bartender, Duane "Guitar Man" Smith of the MisErection- Nig's house band, The Hotslinger twins, Don Dick the Duck Driver, Ned the Giant Winnebago, Wanda Torpedo the Tee-shirt babe, assorted tourists, and Jim the Gunslinger-Photog, who owned the *Old Time Photos* studio next door to Nigs and sometimes got lost. They all disembarked and surrounded Schneider and Liz.

"PARTY!"

"Beautiful fire."

"Nice guitar- mind if I try?"

"Great night for shooting stars."

"Got any weed?"

Schneider hung his head. Liz didn't seem to mind at all. Just then another boat approached. It was the *OKID*. It too slid up on the beach and released the Okids and their guests.

"We saw the boats coming out and figured you were screwed anyway, so here we are," explained Seering.

"Seering, at this rate I'll never...never mind."

The party grew into the biggest one-night fetes in Dells history. Entire trees were felled and thrown on Schneider's little campfire until it grew into a conflagration that washed out the meteor shower everyone had come to see. The scene was now approaching something out of an old *Beach Blanket* movie except for the heavy smog produced by the bonfire and the dope.

Schneider found himself sitting in the sand between Seering and Liz while everyone listened to "Guitar Man" Smith jamming on Schneider's guitar. Schneider noticed Joe Redmund in the crowd.

Joe had his beloved brass lantern with him- the one he kept on the Apollo and used on his bicycle when riding home at night. Redmund's father had given it to him and Joe was proud as hell of it, a family heirloom. The music played on and later Schneider glanced over and saw Ned the Giant Winnebago, now barely functional, taking an interest in Joe's prized lantern.

First Ned looked at it, then picked it up and shook it a little. Then he put it down and started tapping it- just tapping it- with a large rock. Redmund was taking a dip in the river and was oblivious to his impending loss.

Schneider leaned over across Seering and addressed the large Native American.

"Ned, that's not yours."

"Hummph."

"It belongs to Joe Redmund and it's very special to him."

Seering didn't move but muttered something out the corner of his mouth to the effect that Schneider was out of his mind and that they were all going to die.

"Ned, may I see the lantern?"

"No. Goway."

"Please Ned. I need it to see something."

"Oh, Ok." Ned passed the brass lantern across Seering and over to Schneider. The lantern was still working and in its light Seering appeared white as a ghost.

"Thank you, Ned. I'll be right back."

"Don't be long," called Seering.

Schneider delivered the lantern back into Redmund loving hands. Dawn was starting to announce itself and things were getting quiet.

"Thanks,"   Joe   Redmund   told Schneider. "I owe you one."

****

"Silver bells hanging on a string..."

Schneider didn't nap at all that day, and he was a little drowsy by the time for work arrived. He came downstairs wondering what Liz' reaction to the previous night would be. Would she express disappointment that they had been interrupted? Would she thank him for the wonderful time?

Instead, Liz simply said "great party last night, wasn't it?"

She is either the coolest cucumber I have ever met or she just doesn't care, lamented Schneider as they sang their love songs together.

The evening was winding its way into obscurity when five young men walked into the bar, obviously intoxicated, with the intent of sharing "last call" at the River Inn. They requested a couple *Crosby Stills Nash* tunes and then announced that the guy in the middle was being married the following Saturday and that they had just come from his bachelor's party. Schneider sang his version of the Chuck Berry classic *"My Ding-a-ling"* for him and was made an honorary member of the wedding party.

Around bar time an offer was made: would Schneider drive back with them to the bride's hometown- thirty miles distant- and serenade her father with *Ding a ling*?

Schneider hesitated. A hat was passed around. Twice.

They pulled into the sprawling estate around 3:30AM. The groom and his wedding party stumbled up to the door of the huge Tudor-style home and rang the doorbell.

"Doccttorrr S-SSpauldingg, COULD YOU PLEEEASE COME TO THE DOOOOR?" Giggles.

A light appeared in an upstairs window. Schneider took a few steps back. He would have preferred to run back to the River Inn. Too late. Another light appeared in the living room window. Then the porch light. The door opened.

"*WHEN I WAS A LITTLE BITTY BOY, MY GRANDMOTHER BOUGHT ME THIS CUTE LITTLE TOY…*"

Dr. Spaulding didn't look happy. He did, however, know the chorus and joined in before yawning "Ok, boys, you can go home now."

It was the easiest seventy-five bucks Schneider ever made.

****

By the time Schneider got back to the River Inn it was 4AM. He hadn't slept in nearly forty-eight hours. When he walked through the glass doors to go up to his room, he noticed there was lights on in the lounge so he went down to investigate.

What ensued nearly killed him.

He once again found himself sprawled at the bottom of the steep stairway looking up at the bar.

"Godammit! Isn't anyone going to do anything about these step—forget it." He picked himself up once again.

Mike and the River Inn's salad girl were talking at the bar. There were several empty bottles of Coors Light in front of Patty the salad girl and it was obvious she was feeling no pain.

"Evenin' Dave," said Mike. Patty stayed late to help me clean up. I was telling her about the little blast I have planned for next week.

"How about a nightcap?" asked Patty.

"Sure. I'm buying this round," said Schneider. He recounted the *Ding-a ling* story to Mike and Patty. "Looks like you're a little bit ahead of me," Schneider told Patty as he scanned the bottles in front of her.

"Oh, don't let that stop you" she replied. "Tell you what- let's have Mike here line up some shots and I bet I can finish mine before you." Schneider looked across the bar at the cute little blonde-haired Salad Girl. She wouldn't weigh ninety pounds soaking wet. He glanced again at the empty beer bottles on the bar.

"Are you sure you want to do this?" he asked.

"Line 'em up, Mike." She replied.

Mike lined them up.

"Go!" he grinned.

Bang, bang, bang, bang, bang, bang. Schneider downed his last shot of Jack Daniels and looked across at Patty. She was smiling at him with her hands neatly folded on the bar. Every glass in front of her was empty and neatly arranged in a straight line.

"Wake me up in time for Labor Day," managed Schneider before crawling up the steps to his room on hands and knees. He slept for three days.

9

"It was skullduggery just before the Civil War that caused Newport Wisconsin to go bust… Strong personalities and deceptive practices were operating here..."

In his treatise on the Wisconsin River, historian William Stark begins his chapter on Wisconsin Dells with those words.

He goes on to relate the story of Jonathan Bowman and Joseph Bailey and their attempts to build a bridge across the lower Dells at Newport.

He further relates the efforts of Byron Kilbourn, then mayor of Milwaukee, and founder of the local railroad, to thwart that plan as he successfully obtained the rights to the crossing and ultimately built a railroad bridge and dam three miles up-river at a location he unhumbly named Kilbourn City- later to be renamed Wisconsin Dells. Down river, Newport went bust.

Stark continues:

"It was later that an investigation discovered records that nine hundred thousand dollars' worth of bribes were given by Kilbourn... including $175,000 in bonds to Wisconsin's Governor."

It was this kind of intrigue that put Wisconsin Dells on the map- just as surely as the fast water, White Pines and White Sandstone bluffs did. This fact was never lost on the town's locals, and they remain fiercely creative and "*entrepreneurial*" to this day.

At no time is this more evident than Labor Day weekend, when *everything goes* in a town where *anything goes*. It is the annual blow-off of the season; a time for letting one's hair down and rewarding one's self for a job well done while serving the season's visitors (i.e. fleecing the tourists).

It is, at the same time, the busiest weekend of the season, and the wildest. Locals and employees party right alongside their patrons- especially on Monday- and the results can get quite spectacular. It was in this spirit that Mike the Bartender planned his Pre-Labor Day Blast. The event would take place the Tuesday before Labor Day weekend.

Ten half barrels of beer, sixty pounds of dynamite, and nineteen thousand dollars' worth of photo, movie, and video gear, all gathered around one poor, decrepit automobile whose time had come. Schneider woke up just in time.

****

"I don't run from tears,
that's my   weakness- Excuse me..."
-S. Stills

The scene reminded Schneider of Woodstock- a pastoral of rolling hills and farmland filled with an army of people- except that instead of a music stage, the center of attention was a non-descript white Ford Pinto with its hood and trunk open. It sat a hundred yards away from the growing hordes of revelers and was attended by several men with casual clothes but military bearing.

Concentric circles surrounded the car at various distances made up of tripod-mounted Nikons, Hasselblads, and Sonys. A hint of color was starting to show up in the trees beyond the outer circle, a rope with half barrels set up at equal distances along its length. The place was packed. Mike had done his homework.

"I wonder how much he still owes on that car, Schneider asked Liz, looking off towards the Ford.

"Only in the Dells," she responded.

Schneider had given Liz a ride to the big event, hoping this would be their chance to finally "get off the dime." The summer was almost over and he still had no idea where he stood with her.

Maybe that <u>was</u> an indication of how he stood with her, he thought.

"What's the big frown for?" asked Liz.

"I just realized the summer's almost over. That we- the Okids that is-

"Will end?"

"Yeah."

She squeezed his hand. "I don't think you can stop the Okids. They're like a moving train," she laughed.

Yeah, thought Schneider. *Running right over my heart.*

"Testing one, two- *squeeeek.*"

The P.A. came to life. "Hey, everyone! This is Mike. I just wanted to thank y'all for coming. A couple of ground rules before we get started. First, please stay outside the roped-off area. I wouldn't trust most of you with a beer and a boom box much less the gear we have set up here. And of course the guys you see rigging the car have all been a little punch-drunk since 'Nam and I would hate to see any of you get too close to the car in case of a miss-cue. We're going to aim for a three O'clock blast off. We'll give you plenty of warning. In the meantime, be smart and have a good time."

Schneider and Liz saw some familiar faces and walked over to them while discussing the upcoming Labor Day festivities. Seering had planned a rafting party from Stand Rock all the way down to the River Inn for all River Inn employees on Thursday. The bar and dining room would be closed until 5PM so everyone could make it.

The Okids were also planning to get together Monday for a final trip on the OKID and a cookout/ employee party on the River Inn deck afterwards.

They walked over to Joel Ireland, Dave Wright and Randy Highridge.

"Dave, Joel, Randy."

"Liz, Schneidy."

"Think the payment book is really in the glove compartment?"

"Only in the *Dells*" they all muttered, then looked at each other and laughed.

∗∗∗∗∗∗∗∗∗∗∗∗∗∗∗∗∗∗∗∗∗∗∗∗

The forward of Captain Don Saunders' book on the Dells' local myths and Winnebago legends speaks to his own personal connection with the spirit of the place where wave and rock and tall pines meet. He writes

And when I die they must cremate me…pure white ashes, the essence of the little that was good in me. They must take those ashes to Romance Cliff and fling them to the winds and the waters… to blend with the things I love so well forever more.

I would want the summer suns to warm me to the joy of life and love, to the wonders of a canoe skimming 'twixt towered bluffs crowned by emerald and jade. To the thrill of a swim in ambered waters surrounded by singing woodland, turquoise sky and rock giants…

Then just after the death of the flowers, before they are buried in snow, I would want the autumn leaves to embrace me with their glow. Falling leaves to a kindred spirit.

****

Autumn was just around the corner but the sun still warmed the water and the rocks and the Okids.

At 9AM Thursday morning the staff of the River Inn gathered at Stand Rock's dock on the Great Bay to begin their rafting party. Seering had assembled twelve six-man inflatables as well as the *OKID* to act as a floating beer, wine and food pantry. He had taken Debbie Klinke along on the *OKID*, which was a mystery to Schneider- Tammy would certainly be taking part in this little adventure. It wasn't the first time Schneider was confused about such things.

Seering had also made one more tactical error. He had opted for bottles of beer to be brought along on the trip instead of a keg. By 9:30 a flotilla looking something like Castro's bedraggled Mariel Boatlift formed up and started floating down river, joining the tour boats and assorted pleasure craft. Schneider and Seering had a date with destiny that day, but they couldn't know it yet.

The *OKID* was doing a brisk business, serving out beer and wine. Rafts would row over and, by late morning, as the ragtag navy approached the narrows, Patty the salad girl was passed out (how was that possible?) and three inflatables had turned into de-flatables and had dumped twelve employees in the river.

These employees simply swam along with the other rafts while holding their drinks over their heads between gulps. One in particular, a veteran waitress who took great pride in the shape of her middle-aged body, decided she would swim through the narrows. She was an excellent swimmer, Seering agreed, but he was able to convince her to climb aboard one of the other rafts just as the Narrows came into view.

At this point, the exact chain of events becomes a bit sketchy, but this is roughly what happened:

The *OKID* suddenly developed engine trouble and its 40 horse Mercury sputtered out, leaving it a floating raft like the others.

Schneider joins Seering and Debbie Klinke onboard the *OKID* to see if he can help. Dan and Debbie start arguing about- what else- other women.

Seering decides he doesn't want to make a scene and spies Tammy and "The Maid" in a nearby raft. He immediately abandons ship and makes his way to the raft. Klinke is *really* pissed. So is Schneider, since he wants to swim over to Liz and can't as long as he is needed on- board the *OKID*.

Without the noise of the *OKID*'s outboard, things suddenly seem very quiet. Schneider looks around and is stunned at the scene behind him. A floating trail of beer bottles, deflated rubber rafts, and drunken employees accompany the flotilla. Things are getting a bit out of control.

At that moment three distant horn blasts grab Schneider's attention. It occurs to him what is happening and he looks down at his watch, afraid of what he'll see.

His worst fears are realized.

It is 12:15. Those three blasts are from the *Clipper Winnebago* as she enters the narrows from the down- river side. The *Okid*- now without power- and the rest of the flotilla is approaching from the up-river side. In five minutes they will converge at the Elbow.

****

"Seering," hailed Schneider. "Seering- did you hear that?"

Seering didn't even hear Schneider, as he was engrossed in conversation with Tammy and the Maid.

"SEEEEERING!!"

"Jeeesus, whaaat Schneids- can't you see I'm busy?"

"Please... come...here- I want to talk to youuuuu."

"Nooooooooooo."

"SEERING   GET   YOUR MISERABLE ASS OVER HERE- NOW! - THE *CLIPPER'S* COMING!"

Schneider could see Seering look at his watch.

"H-O-L-Y SHIT!!"

Seering dove in and swam over.

"What do we do now, Captain?" asked Schneider as Seering pulled himself aboard.

"Carry on--as you were-- make it so..."

"Oh, shit...."

The *OKID,* twelve rafts in assorted stages of buoyancy and forty-five employees in similar shape approached the elbow's ninety-degree turn.

The bow and pilothouse of the *Clipper* seemed to grow huge and loom out of the rock walls to the right. It started to turn into the elbow and headed straight for them. Four blasts of its horn signaled the standard emergency call known to all mariners-

meaning "get out of the way/ a collision is imminent."

"Dell's Boat Company is not gonna like us scraping their pretty rocks and getting yellow paint all over them," Schneider said in a low nervous tone. He and Seering grabbed whatever they could to use as paddles and tried to get the doomed pontoon boat over to the side of the river.

Suddenly, five blasts echoed through the chasm and something occurred that Seering couldn't remember ever seeing in ten years on the river- *The Clipper Winnebago* started to *back up*- right in the middle of the Elbow. Unheard of- and very dangerous. That gave Seering and Schneider the time they needed to find a little nook in the stone walls in which to guide the little yellow pontoon boat out of harm's way. The *Clipper* once again came ahead and passed the *OKID* with assorted ominous looks and gestures. Seering looked at Schneider. Schneider looked at Seering.

They continued to bump and crawl their way through the narrows and emerged with their band of ragtag gypsies at Black Hawk Island, where a D.B.C. boat met them to chew them out and tow them all to the

River Inn in time for work. That is, after the Okids picked up the beer bottles and deflated rubber floating from Stand Rock to Black Hawk Island.

****

Friday evening signaled the official opening of the Labor Day weekend celebration, which would culminate with "Locals Play day" on Monday. By Tuesday, the tourists would be gone, and the summer help off to college or other work.

Schneider was happy to see a lot of regulars, all in their "assigned seats" when he came downstairs and into the lounge for work. Mayor Colsen and the rest of the *Dells' Mafia* sat commiserating over their weekly Friday golf outing, waiting for dinner over double scotches by the windows.

Stan and Fran had picked this weekend for their late summer vacation binge and were sitting at the bar behind shot glasses and beer. Wright sat next to them by the waitress station sipping a Windsor on the rocks.

It was 7:00PM. Schneider had asked Liz to have dinner with him that night, and she had gotten permission from Seering to take a long break in the dining room.

She was singing a song Schneider hadn't heard before, so Schneider sat and listened. The song said it all.

She must have written it, thought Schneider, *but did she write it for me?*

At their usual place on the end of the bar sat Frank Allison and Joe Redmund, both with soft drinks in front of them. They were probably killing some time, waiting for the steam to come up in the *Apollo* before setting off on their dinner cruise up to Stand Rock. Schneider had had an idea in mind ever since earning Redmund' gratitude at the Bare Ass Beach all-nighter. He walked over to them.

"Frank, Joe."

"Evenin' Schneidy"

"Joe, Frank, I'm not sure how to ask this, and if you feel uncomfortable about it just tell me, but there is something I would love to try this weekend." Schneider told them what it was.

"It's never been done before," smiled Allison as he thought. "*You* might be able to do it though, he said, eyeing Schneider up and down. "I bet we could fit that in Monday. What do you think Joe?"

Redmund smiled, giggled, and then nodded. They finished their Cokes. Allison glanced out the window toward the Apollo's dock.

"We gotta go. You get the stuff and we'll make it happen. Sounds like a hell of an addition to Monday's activities, Dave."

As they walked away, Schneider could hear Frank Allison ask Joe Redmund "What's gone with that boy, I wonder?"

****

"Evenin' Dave."

"Hey Schneidy," answered Wright as Schneider approached. "What's happening?"

"Having dinner with Liz. Seering told her she could take some time tonight."

"Sounds like he's rooting for you too. How's it going?"

"With Liz you mean?"

Wright nodded.

"I still don't know."

Wright shrugged. "I've known women- usually beautiful women- who will absolutely not hint at their affections until the man makes an obvious move. They figure the guy has to *earn* the shot."

"Well, that's a tightrope," replied Schneider. "A gentleman doesn't make that move until receiving some cue- verbal, physical- that it may be OK, right? I've received no such clues."

Wright shrugged again. "I'm hardly qualified to comment. I'm on my umpteenth drink of the summer trying to figure out what happened with Kerri."

"Kerri's   Kerri,"   volunteered Schneider, hoping that would be enough.

"Well Liz is definitely worth the effort," said Wright. "Did you hear that last song she just did? Did she write that?"

"Don't know. I'll ask her though. By the way, the River Inn sale fell through. Seering said Klinke couldn't go through with it with those guys from Cleveland."

"Good for him. Someone else will step up. Ever figure out where those mysterious barrels came from?"

"No."

Liz finished her set and walked over.

"Hi Dave, hi Schneidy- ready?"

"You want to join us, Dave?" asked Schneider, knowing the answer.

"No thanks, Nemo's joining me in a few minutes."

Schneider and Liz walked into the dining room and Kerri took them to a small corner table next to the windows. Apparently, everyone was rooting for them.

"I heard your new song just now, opened Schneider. "Beautiful- did you write that?"

"Um-hmm," nodded Liz.

Schneider waited for more but received nothing.

"What was the inspiration?" he asked, growing bolder. Liz was more beautiful tonight than ever. She had on a turquoise print sundress that hinted of a Native American origin and she wore a tiny, yellow feather in her hair. Schneider complimented her.

"In honor of my last weekend in the land of Okids and Winnebagos," she smiled and let slip the cute little giggle that Schneider had grown to love. Schneider could feel his heart melting. He suddenly felt very, very warm.

****

Sunday afternoon. One day to go. The river was full of holiday boat traffic under a clear blue sky. Monday would see the final blowout; then it would be back to Madison and school for Schneider and the girls, where the spring semester was starting. The tourists would leave in time to be back at their jobs by Tuesday morning. The River rats would paint and haul their boats, the shopkeepers would roll back their hours, and the circus would enter semi-hibernation.

Patches of amber and crimson grew larger between the river bluff's white pines.

Once again Seering appeared on the rooftop deck of the River Inn with a six-pack of St. Pauli Girl and a clip- board.

"Time to write?" asked Schneider, looking up from his book.

"This one's gotta be ready tonight," nodded Seering.   Schneider started to read:

She dances under the moon, presses her face to the wind
My brown-eyed daisy is free, running and laughing
Nights- they never end, they all grow into morning
She dances to Desert Skies; all look and laugh and love...

It was for Tammy.

Schneider stopped reading and looked up.

"Seering, how can this be ready for tonight?"

"Dave, Tammy's family is coming tonight. I want you to sing it for her when they're here."

Schneider studied Seering for a moment. "Let's get to work," he said as he reached for a beer and his guitar.

****

"Well I'll be damned, here comes your ghost again, but that's not unusual- it's just that the moon is full and you happen to call…"
                                   - J. Baez

That night Schneider sang his song for Liz. The River Inn was packed. All the regulars were there plus Tammy's family. Unfortunately for Seering, so was Debbie Klinke. Seering had told Schneider he would see her and break it off that night after work but she had circumvented his plans and had shown up early. Now she was sitting with Dave Wright at the bar, fuming.

Wright sipped his Canadian whiskey.

"How can he do this? She's just a child," lamented Debbie.

"Are you upset at the prospect of losing Dan or just pissed off at the competition?" asked Wright. Brutally honest.

"I've been completely faithful to him, the little prick."

I'm sorry, Debbie, but I think he's been faithful to you in his own way. Did he ever try to hide his friendship with Tammy?"

"No."

Wright took another slow sip.

"He's still a shit."

"You know," said Wright, "most people talk a big game about how healthy it is to date different people, but you seldom see it happen without nasty labels being thrown at the people who do it."

She ignored him. "I'm going up to Nigs," she finally said, and walked to the stairs. Wright watched her go. He really did feel sorry for her, but she was never the victim of any deception. And neither was he.

Up near the stage sat Nemo, Joel, Tammy, and Tammy's family. Kathy was on duty 'til 10:00PM, then she would join them. Wright and Joel were there too, ready to play the last set with Schneider. They had become the River Inn's unofficial house band. Seering popped in and out, spending what time he could.

Around 11:00 Seering played what would be the first of many end-of-season practical jokes on Schneider. At exactly the top of the hour, Schneider started a new set and as he played his first chord, the entire lounge- everyone in it- stood up and vacated the premises. As Mayor Bernie Colsen passed a bewildered Schneider on his way out, he muttered "The entertainment sucks here. We're going up to Chula Vista."

"SEERING PUT YOU UP TO THIS DIDN'T HE?!" whined Schneider as Stan and Fran and Nemo and Tammy and the rest of the patrons paraded by. It was 11:20 before anybody returned. They all did however, and the party shifted into high gear.

Later Schneider sang *Brown Eyed Daisy* and Tammy cried and Seering's stock with her and her family went way up. *If only that could happen with Liz*, thought

Schneider. He took a break before calling up Wright and Joel. As they were taking out their instruments and tuning up, Liz approached and asked Schneider if she could sit in too. Schneider said of course and Liz kissed him on the cheek and whispered a thank-you for the song he had wrote for her.

Schneider and Liz, backed up by the Bad Bananas, did every love song they knew that night, followed by the traditional Okid closing triad of My Way, Dessert Skies, and Amazing Grace. Schneider then finished with an Okid Yellow encore. As everyone was clapping, Schneider summoned the courage to give Liz a quick peck on the lips. To his surprise she returned his kiss, albeit very shortly. By the time we leave tomorrow night, thought Schneider, I have GOT to tell her how I feel about her. Of course, in many ways, he already had.

****

The evening wore on, and Schneider stopped playing around bar-time, but everyone stayed- as if afraid to succumb to the relentless clock ticking down towards the end of the summer, the end of an era. Soft conversation ensued until a pink sliver above the river appeared through the picture windows and started to grow into light, once again revealing rising steam and tiny green specks flowing down-river past the River Inn. It was Monday.

Tomorrow at this time, in this place, thought Schneider, we'll all be ghosts.

10

And so it happened that nobody, appropriately, entered Monday's Labor Day celebration with any sleep. Schneider wanted to get started on his plans with Allison and Redmund early, so he set out to get the gear he'd need.

The OKID was scheduled to leave immediately after the breakfast shift, the dining room being closed for the rest of the day.

Schneider got what he needed, dropped it off at the Apollo and was back at the River Inn dock in time to help load up the *OKID*. He hoped Redmund and Allison would remember they were meeting him at noon at Bare Ass Beach.

Schneider couldn't put his finger on it, but there was something in the air this morning. It wasn't a noise; wasn't a scent or a feeling. It was more of a charge- like static electricity. It caused the hairs on his arms to stand up. Nothing *seemed* out of the ordinary-yet. But it promised to get weird- this was Labor Day in Wisconsin Dells, Wisconsin.

Nemo and Ryker were already busy provisioning the *Okid* when Schneider arrived at the dock.

"Dale, Nemo."

"Mornin' Schneids."

"Schneidy. Seering had some office stuff to finish up. He'll be down in a minute."

From the River Inn docks they could see   Broadway's river bridge was already busy with out-bound traffic- as if the tourists knew that this day was reserved for the locals and chose to "get out of Dodge" early. Some, however, chose to stay and join in. By late afternoon, only the hardy would remain.

Soon Tammy and Kathy arrived, and Liz not too long after that. Joel strolled down with his guitar and Wright showed up as well, choosing to come into town for the day rather than be picked up by boat.

Seering finally arrived and the *Okid* shoved off for its final ride of the season, carrying passengers, some of whom didn't know each other three months ago but were now very, very close.

Just up-river from the elbow, at a little bend where Chula Vista sat on the bluffs amidst the pines, Wright announced he had some bottle rockets and that they should be used to entertain "Chula's" well-heeled clientele. A makeshift launching tube was erected on board and some very healthy fireworks began to ascend on the bluffs at Chula Vista.

As the Okid turned to depart the little cove, Kathy could smell something burning. They turned to see one of the oldest, largest white pines on the property awash in flames.

Seering immediately gunned the boat for shore while screaming epitaphs at Wright and his penchant for pyrotechnics. Luckily there were two fire extinguishers on board and between them, and an Okid bucket brigade stretching from the river to the top of the bluff, the fire was extinguished before any major damage could ensue (or any charges be brought by the owners of Chula Vista).

The *Okid* continued its sojourn. Around 11:30am Schneider mentioned that he had to meet the Apollo at Bare Ass Beach at noon. He didn't say why, but Seering got him there in time with the Apollo already there and Allison and Redmund waiting and ready.

****

"HIT IT!" yelled Schneider. All at once the stern of the Apollo became a thundering waterfall and Schneider's world turned into a cross between a ride on the outside of a submarine and the inside of a washer-dryer.

The activity on Bare Ass Beach paused while folks waited to see the first human being in The Dells water-skiing behind a paddlewheel steamboat. Allison blew the whistle when Schneider finally emerged from the foam and stood up. The ride didn't last long, too slow to easily glide over the water, but Schneider clenched his fist during a most exhilarating tumble back into the river. He felt more alive at that moment than any time in his life.

****

The Okids played their last game of volleyball of the summer and left Bare Ass Beach for the River Inn, where employees were gathering for the barbecue. As the *OKID*

headed down-river, carrying friends that couldn't imagine not knowing one another ninety days ago, with the River Inn ahead of them and a summer full of memories behind, Liz pulled out her guitar and sang a song that would stay with Schneider forever. It was the new one she had played the previous evening. After the song, she slipped him a cassette tape of her music.

"This is for you, Schneidy," she whispered.

****

The *OKID* approached the dock at the River Inn. Dale Ryker stepped out to tie her up and, being slightly inebriated stumbled and hit his head on a piling. It required 12 stitches at the local emergency room, but despite the brisk business going on there, Ryker managed to get his face fixed and get back to the party quickly.

While the steaks were grilling and the Bad Bananas were pounding out *Desert Skies*, Seering and Ryker decided that a leap from the rooftop deck to the river would be a good way to celebrate the end of the season. Ken Klinke forbade it, citing Ryker's injury and blocking the way. Seering went left, Ryker went right and together they split Klinke's defense and jumped off the roof.

Unfortunately, Seering's detour took him through the big white pine tree and Ryker drove *him* to the hospital. Eight stitches were required but no bones were broken. They were both back in forty minutes.

****

"Goodnight Sweetheart, it's time to go..."

After the barbecue it was up to Broadway and Nigs Bar for the traditional Labor Day Bloody Marys. Nigs opened at 7am every Labor Day and served half price

Bloody Marys throughout the day for the locals. Strange behavior often resulted. The Okid ranks had thinned by late afternoon, but seven remained: Seering, Tammy, Nemo, Kathy, Liz, Ryker and Schneider.

When they arrived at Nigs, Jim the Gunslinger was wandering around with his empty (hopefully) replica Winchester carbine, and Claire the bartender was still up to her ponytail in Bloody Marys. The Okids sat near a window so they would have a clear view of Broadway. It was quite a show.

Every now and then a Duck would zoom past- with one or more occupants naked. One beat-up Oldsmobile pulled a skateboarder until halted by a local constable.

Several Ducks went by with live music on board. Out of one flew plastic Indian spears and rubber arrows. Schneider watched it all. He was trying not to think about what was coming- saying goodbye to Liz. They were both going to the University next semester, but Schneider still knew it wouldn't be the same. He envied Seering and Ryker, who would be staying on at the River Inn through the off-season. What he didn't know was that Seering envied *him* for being able to go back to Madison. After all, Tammy was going to school there too.

The Mis-Erection started a new set and they all got up to dance. Schneider saw a lot of eyes following Liz around the dance floor. And why not? She looked fabulous in jeans. When a slow number came up, he couldn't believe how wonderful she felt in his arms and how lucky he felt to be her partner, if only for a moment. There was still no hint towards any desire for intimacy, however, so Schneider tried to keep his distance. If only she could be the secret admirer.

God, she smelled good up close.

****

As the autumn color progresses and the thermometer starts to drop, Wisconsin Dells' population decreases by two-thirds. Many of the town's permanent residents will go on unemployment or find work at the core businesses in town; the schools, the Post Office, the Five and Dime, Ken Klinke's grocery store. Many drive truck, due to Wisconsin Dells' proximity to several major freeways.

The river rats will spend the fall fixing and hauling the boats, then blend into the winter landscape, to once again re-emerge in the spring.

Several resorts and bars will stay open, dispensing temporary shelter and hot toddies to the frozen locals as well as the occasional skier or snowmobiler.

Most of the better restaurants in town will stay open, as well as the *Dells Grill*, without which half the town residents would never eat breakfast. The *Friday Fish Fry* will once again become the Locals' big evening out.

Down on the river, the ice will start forming in the Great Bay and move downstream as the winter progresses. Eventually, the only open water remaining will be beneath the dam. That's when the eagles will come to fish. Further downstream, the abandoned town of Newport will lie under a blanket of snow until the vintage Ducks once again carry tourists over its old roadbeds. The white pines will provide shelter for a multitude of wildlife and the red sandstone bluffs will turn black against the winter's snow.

Schneider and most of the Okids will return during the next few months and renew friendships over hot buttered rums and warm spiced tea around Seering's old wood burner. The River Inn will remain under the same ownership. The frost will return to the River Inn's French doors but will merely serve to warm the Okids' spirits. The Okids will all vow to return in the spring.

They will all keep their promises.

****

A moment in time

Goodnight world, its time to go
To where or what we do not know
A distant shore or newfound land
Perhaps to walk on hand in hand

The day is night once again
Leaving behind a thought in mind
That all that's been or ever been known
Comes taken from a page- a moment in time

This moment in time is a registered deed
Risen from Spring's delicate seed
To taste the hope and pick from the vine
To say it was moment in time

Forever fades and stories end
The waters mix but never blend
And what is, is not- we finally find
that what is- is actually a moment in time
                                   - Seering

At this moment in time, the light of Labor Day was growing dim and it became time to go. The group of seven near the windows at Nigs became strangely silent. Liz was the first to get up. Her car was in the parking lot and she was already overdue in Madison.

"I'll walk you out," said Schneider. Liz hugged everyone and then offered Schneider her hand on the way out. Schneider stopped short of Liz's car.

"I don't want this to end," he told her. Then he pulled her close and kissed her.

"See ya, Schneidy. Thanks for the song."

"Yeah... See ya, Liz.

And then she was gone. By the time he got back to the table, Wright and Joel and Wanda the tee-shirt babe had joined them. The party was still growing, but Schneider felt completely alone. Tammy and Seering were talking quietly while holding hands. Kathy sat on Nemo's lap. Neither spoke.

The band played on.

_11_

*"Summer's gone like the faded songs
that meant so much to me..."*
                                        - D. Seering

Schneider decided to leave in the morning. He should have been fortified by a wonderful day and the possibility of more to come with Liz. But still he felt depressed. He was certain nothing would come of it. Although it had felt wonderful, it hadn't felt *right*.

When he got back to the River Inn, he walked in the lounge entrance and smiled at the stairway from hell that he had walked (or fallen) up and down so many times that summer. He smiled as he looked out the windows, the river view now illuminated by outdoor floodlights. He smiled, remembering seeing Liz that first time from this same spot. He walked upstairs to his room and slid the cassette tape that Liz had given him into his stereo. He fast-forwarded to the song he needed to hear- the one she had sung for him that afternoon:

Where did all the time go?
Why did it go so fast?
Seems like it slipped through our fingers
and went right past

What happened to all my memories
The ones I held so dear
Thought I'd always keep them close at hand
Keep them near

But I'll remember cool cotton mornings
Silky sunny afternoons
Blue satin evenings turned to midnight
I'll remember you.

But now it's time to say goodbye my friend
We always knew there would come a day
Good things must come to an end so they say
But can you tell me where did all the time
go?
                                        -Liz Kinstler

He let the song play out, then pushed *rewind* and went to pull down the sheets of his bed. As he did, a book fell to the floor. Schneider had never seen it before.

It was collection of letters and other writings of Vincent van Gogh, collected by Vincent's brother Theo. The book was open to a particular page and a passage was highlighted.

Schneider read:

"I would rather die of passion than of boredom."

In the margin Seering had scribbled:

Here's to fighting the good fight.
Goodnight, Schneids.

Author's Note

There really is a Wisconsin Dells. All characters and occurrences, while based on my experiences and the extraordinary friendships forged there, are fictitious.

Nothing in this story or setting should be construed as historically or geographically accurate except where annotated.

By the way, I married the cocktail waitress. Smartest thing I did in my whole life. She actually played a much larger role in my first Dells year, but like I said, I am only telling a story here.

First thanks must go to Dan Seering, the only surname I didn't change. Sorry, Seering- it just wouldn't work with any name but yours. Incidentally, I stole a lot of material for this from his book Remember the Time? Many thanks to Dave Knight, Tom Butler and others who gave me helpful advice.

I also wish to thank Mike Baumgartner of Dells Boat Tours and Paul Herr of Nature Safaris, for their expertise on the area, as well as Don Saunders, William Stark, and Daniel Dahlquist. If you get a chance, read their work.

My biggest thanks go to Layna and to Rose, my heroes of the real, true story.

Finally, if you ever get a chance to visit the Dells, or any small tourist town like it, I encourage you to do so like a native; get off the beaten path. Talk to the locals. Search for the soul of the place...

and never, ever follow the billboards.

Just listen to the wind blow...

- David Schneider

Made in the USA
Las Vegas, NV
23 March 2021